PROMISE ME
the MOON

JOYCE ANNETTE BARNES

Dial Books for Young Readers   New York

Published by Dial Books for Young Readers
A Division of Penguin Books USA Inc.
375 Hudson Street / New York, New York 10014

Designed by Pamela Darcy
Printed in the U.S.A. on acid-free paper / First Edition
1   3   5   7   9   10   8   6   4   2

Library of Congress Cataloging in Publication Data
Barnes, Joyce Annette.
Promise me the moon / Joyce Annette Barnes.—1st ed.
p.   cm.
Summary: Thirteen-year-old Annie wonders about her dream of
becoming an astronaut as she faces various challenges and self-
doubts, including changes in her relationship with her best friend,
fights with her parents, and problems at school.
ISBN 0-8037-1798-9 (trade).
[1. Afro-Americans—Fiction.   2. Parent and child—Fiction.
3. Self-realization—Fiction.   4. Schools—Fiction.]   I. Title.
PZ7.B2624Pr   1997
[Fic]—dc20   95-53085   CIP   AC

Excerpts from *To Be Young, Gifted and Black* by Lorraine Hansberry,
adapted by Robert Nemiroff (Englewood Cliffs, NJ: Prentice-Hall, Inc.,
1969) appear by permission of Random House, Inc.

Acknowledgments

*Thanks to Mary Jack Wald for encouraging me from the very beginning and to
Cindy Kane for her excellent editorial advice. Thanks to Laurie Murdock-West
for help with terminology, and to James M. Thornton in Dayton, Ohio, for scientific information. In particular, I thank my children, Justin, Malik, and
Pilar; my family and friends; and my husband, David Barnes, all of whom
have given me freedom and time to write. And most of all, thank you to my
mother, Frances Moore, for giving me life and love and a passion for
reading and writing.*

*To my father, John W. Moss,
and other fathers who work too much
because they love us*

PART ONE

Separate Ways

1

Labor Day is supposed to be the official end of summer. School starts tomorrow, but it's hard to shift into pupil mode on a day like today, eighty-eight degrees and brilliantly sunny.

I'm starting to feel like a baked potato, sitting on my front porch in this heat, waiting for Claude. We have a job to do this afternoon and he's late. I start to think I should just go on without him. But I don't. I sit there in the glare of the sun, getting warmer and angrier by the second.

Down the street four little girls play jump rope like they've been doing every day since school let out. Carmelita skipping the rope, Renee and Sweet Pea turning, and little Anita on the side, bobbing her head in time, all of them singing: *"One day in the middle of June, a boy named Jerome! promised me the moon . . ."*

The jumping girl squeals at the boy the others chose

for her, pretending she doesn't like him, the way I used to do when someone would yell out *Claude!* for my turn. Carmelita misses, and, automatically, they move to their new positions and start the rhythm again. Not a care in the world except whose turn is next.

I miss being a kid.

The sun shines relentlessly. I check the crude sundial Claude and I put up in my front yard. Almost three o'clock. I lie back against the concrete porch and let out a long, deep sigh.

I've been sighing a lot lately. I like doing it. I can feel consoled and tragic at the same time. I sigh a few more times.

In between, I listen to my father's snores coming through the screen door. It's a holiday, so my parents are off from work. A rare event. Daddy got up at seven this morning, had his ribs and hot dogs barbecued well before noon. Now he's two beers into a deep sleep on the living room couch. From her perch in her chair, her legs kicked up on a footstool, Mama leisurely turns the pages of *Ebony* magazine, reading every article to the end instead of rushing over the paragraphs like she usually does. They sound at ease, unusual for them. How sad that they have to wait until the last official day of summer to relax. I sigh again.

Finally, Claude appears on his front porch. He looks across the street and waves at me like nothing's wrong. I take my time waving back. Standing, I call, "I'm gone!" to Mama through the screen.

Sometimes I think my mother has superhuman powers. She's at the door in a flash, before I can take two steps off the porch. "Where're you going, Annie?"

I wish I had bet someone a hundred dollars because I knew she was going to ask me that. Even though I told her last night exactly what Claude and I have to do today.

"To Mr. Blackstone's house," I say with an attitude, "to move the boxes. *Remember?*"

Mama decides it's too much of an attitude. "Watch your tone, girl."

"Yes, ma'am," I reply before escaping out of the yard. It's too hot to get into it with my mother.

Claude watches me cross the street, then meets me on the sidewalk and slips his arms around my waist. "Claude," I whisper, pulling away, "Mama's standing at the door." His hands and grin drop immediately. He hates to be caught doing something he's not supposed to do. He wants all the grown-ups to keep their excellent opinion of him. Mama likes Claude, but he doesn't fool her. She periodically reminds me, "Claude is fifteen years old, Annie, and you're only thirteen."

He may be older than me, but Claude and I are in love. We've been going out for two years, ever since he bought me ten birthstone rings from Mr. Hershey's store, one for each finger. The rings all broke after about a month, but Claude and I stayed together. He runs cross-country for Walker High School, and he's smart. He's the color of sand and he's got big soulful-looking eyes. And he's the only boy I know who doesn't think I'm crazy for wanting to be an astronaut, because that's also what he wants to be. We're going to become NASA pilots and fly to the moon one day. Together. I think going to the moon with Claude is the best thing that could happen to me.

Claude tries to smile and play it off. He whispers, "Let's go," as if she could hear him if he spoke in a normal voice. Knowing my mother, maybe she could. I stifle a giggle and, in stride, Claude and I turn left at the end of our street. We both throw a hand across our eyes against the sun and start the climb toward the place where Oakwood, our neighborhood, begins: Mr. Otis Blackstone's house.

"What took you so long?" I ask after a while.

"I had a telephone call. Business. Mr. B. will understand." He has the nerve to look annoyed, when I'd been the one getting cooked out in the hot sun. He waits for me to ask him about this "business." Ever since he found out Mr. Blackstone's family used to run their own company, Claude finds any opportunity he can to talk with him about business. Like he's some CEO out here in the world and Mr. Blackstone is Chairman of the Board.

I let the subject drop.

We used to think Oakwood ended at Mr. Blackstone's house, but now we know his was the first house built in the neighborhood, on the first street. I pause before opening the eight-foot-tall, wrought-iron front gate. Even though I come here almost every week, I can't help feeling a little awed every time by Mr. Blackstone's mansion of a house. It's not really a mansion, but it does have seven bedrooms, a kitchen as big as a studio apartment, and forty windows. His grandparents built the place in 1858, after they escaped from slavery in Virginia and ended up here, in Ohio. They traveled the Underground Railroad (which when I was little I thought was a subway train). Later, they helped other people escape and hid them in their big house. This house.

I don't know. Sometimes when I look up from the gate, it seems like those escaped slaves are staring at me out of every one of those forty windows. Despite the heat, I get a chill just thinking about them.

Mr. Blackstone's niece Amanda, frowning as usual, answers our knock. She moved in with her widowed uncle about a year ago and now apparently considers herself some kind of palace guard. "He's in the parlor, asleep," she says, crossing her arms, blocking our way.

Claude explains, putting on his best I'm-a-good-kid manners: "We're supposed to move those old trunks and boxes from the attic, Miss Amanda." She twists her face into a deeper frown, looks back and forth at us, then silently steps back and lets us in. Amanda retreats down the hall, mumbling. She closes the kitchen door, muffling the smell of brewing coffee and the sound of gospel music on the radio.

Mr. Blackstone is not asleep. He's sitting in the shadows cast through the long windows along one side of the room. All the lamps are off. I think Mr. Blackstone likes his house a little gloomy, to remind him of something sad—his wife's death, maybe, even though it was so long ago. I'll bet he sighs deeply in here.

He's settled into his favorite parlor chair, the one right under his wife's portrait, and rests his feet on the matching stool. Despite the heat, an afghan is thrown over his lap. His pale wrinkled face creases into a deep smile when he sees us. "I thought I had lost you both to the beautiful summer day."

"See, Claude," I say accusingly.

"I was late," Claude admits, then adds, "but it was for a good reason. Come on, Annie. Let's get started."

I pointedly take a seat and ignore him. "Mr. Blackstone," I say, "can you believe it's the end of summer break. School starts tomorrow. Where *did* the time go?"

Mr. Blackstone runs his hand across his smooth white hair, clipped short thanks to Amanda. He is eighty-six years old, but he has what my grandmother calls "a young heart." He plays along. "Yes, indeed, Miss Armstrong. Tell me now, was it a good summer?"

"Oh, well, I met a wonderful boy. Very smart, you know," I reply with a mock British accent. "But with no manners. Why, he thinks he can just come to someone's house and not have a visit."

Mr. Blackstone goes *tsk tsk*. Claude pulls me out of the chair. "We'll visit later, Mr. B. Got something to discuss with you anyway. Business," he emphasizes, like he's referring to something way over my head.

What's he up to? I wonder, letting him lead me out of the room.

To get to the attic, we have to go up the kitchen stairs. Amanda, mixing cake frosting, abruptly turns off her blender and halts our progress across the room.

"We know what to do, Miss Amanda," says Claude. "Annie and I discovered those boxes, remember?"

"I don't care who found what. If you ask me, you shouldn't be rooting around up there. Ought to leave the past alone. Just 'cause *she* say you ought to do it, don't mean you ought to do it. Why these people around here think they have to jump every time *she* say jump, I don't know—"

The *she* Amanda so bitterly refers to is Miss Evangeline, our nosiest neighbor. Miss Evangeline is a widow, but we still call her *Miss*. She's the bossiest lady we know, always ordering people around. She missed her calling as a drill sergeant. She's a big woman too, solid. Until we discovered Mr. Blackstone, we thought she was our richest neighbor. So did she. Miss Evangeline lets everyone know how much influence, and money, she has. And she's always riled up about something, like if people let their grass grow too high or don't paint their houses.

Now she's just rhapsodic about the Blackstone house. Miss Evangeline and some other civic-minded ladies in the neighborhood started the Oakwood Restoration Project just to get it declared a historic monument. She's talked to the mayor, the city council, anybody she could think of, and they've all said she needs more documentation, more proof that there is history worth restoring. So, of course, Miss Evangeline drafted Claude and me to move some old boxes downstairs so that she can look for that proof.

We don't mind doing the work. We want to know what she comes up with. Maybe there's some treasure hidden in Mr. Blackstone's house. Or at least some juicy secrets.

Amanda breaks off her tirade and remembers why she stopped us. "You need a scarf for your head, Annie," she scolds, just like she's my aunt or somebody. "You'll come out of there covered in dust. I know your mama didn't pay good money to get your hair done so you could dirty it up over here—"

She leads us up the back steps, gets a bandanna from her bedroom on the second floor, and ties it snugly over my head. We laugh at my Aunt Jemima look, but before she can get back down the stairs, she's complaining again: "—carting that old junk out just because *she*—"

When she leaves, I roll one finger around on the side of my head. "Crazy."

"Yeah," Claude agrees. "Come on."

I follow him down the hallway to the closed attic door. Claude unlocks the door with the skeleton key hanging on a string around the doorknob. When the door opens, a blast of dusty, hot air hits us, sending me into a sneezing fit. "Bless you," he says when it's over. Then he pushes the light switch on. For a second the bulb above us flickers, but then something buzzes and in the next second, everything goes dark and quiet. A smell like burned acid hits our noses.

Amanda's radio and mixer have cut off in the kitchen. "What are you children *doing* up there?"

We cover our mouths so she won't hear us laughing. Claude yells back, "It's probably just a fuse, Miss Amanda. I'll fix it." He asks me, "You coming?"

He means the basement, a moldy, musty, dark cavern. I dislike basements. I dislike dark places. But I go downstairs with him anyway.

Amanda watches skeptically as we reach the top of the basement steps. "Do y'all know what you're doing?"

"Sure, Miss Amanda," I answer because Claude has already grabbed the flashlight hanging on the wall and started down. Truth is, I've never changed, or even seen, a fuse, but I'm following Claude and he seems to know what he's doing.

The flashlight has a wide face and a full circle of light, wider than the steps. But once downstairs, it's nowhere near enough to light the whole basement. This place is long and wide, empty and dark. A chill tickles my spine. I grab onto the back of Claude's shirt and walk close behind him. In the middle of the room, he stops suddenly, turns around to face me, and clicks off the flashlight. The hair on my arms stands on end.

"Claude!" I gasp. "What happened to the light?"

"Nothing, Annie. Just be cool." He puts his arms around my waist again, reaches his face to mine, and kisses me.

I like kissing Claude. I've kept a record of every time we've kissed, exactly twelve times since the launching of *Apollo 11* in 1969. This time makes thirteen. But it feels too eerie kissing down here in this basement.

I squirm away. "Turn on the light. Please."

"Sshh. It's okay, Annie."

"Amanda's gonna wonder what we're doing down here."

"But she can't see." He laughs and reaches to kiss me again. This time, his hands grope for the top button of my shirt, which he loosens before I even realize what he's doing.

I pull away and hastily rebutton it, surprised at Claude. He's never tried anything like that before.

"Turn on the light. I'm going back upstairs."

"Don't be such a baby, Annie," his voice comes to me out of the dark. "Grow up."

I don't feel like being teased. I hate being called names, even by Claude. I try to sound more firm. "Turn it on. Now!"

Before the words are out of my mouth, I sense movement over my foot. Something low and thick and furry rubs against my left ankle and is gone so fast that by the time Claude clicks the flashlight on, all we can see is a long, flippy tail disappearing down a hole.

"*Ulp!*" I yell, "a rat, a rat!" I start screaming like a madwoman, clutching my ankle, rubbing furiously to get rid of the slimy, furry sensation. "Get it off me, Claude, get it off!"

"It's gone, Annie," Claude insists, trying in vain to get me to calm down.

"No, I still feel it. Get it off! Get it off!!"

Miss Amanda and Mr. Blackstone call anxiously from the top of the steps. "What's happened? What's going on?"

"A rat! a rat! a rat!" I scream repeatedly. "Oh, it *rubbed up against my leg!*" Shock waves of revulsion sweep through me. Finally, Claude picks me up and practically carries me up the steps.

In the kitchen my screams turn to whimpering and tears, and then just whimpering. I feel like I'm gonna throw up. I hold my stomach and sit doubled over in the chair.

Amanda, glad to be able to blame Miss Evangeline for something else, says, "Y'all shouldn't have been down there in the first place. That Evangeline shouldn't have you messing around in this place."

Mr. Blackstone looks me over, concern creasing his face. "I'll hire professional movers. You children shouldn't be put in danger. We'll let someone else handle it."

"No!" Claude says, and I find myself agreeing with him.

"I'm okay," I manage to say. I don't want Mr. Blackstone to lose confidence in us. "I'm sorry I screamed. But it—" I cringe all over again, "it rubbed up against me!"

"Dear child." He pats my back. "Nobody's blaming you."

"Besides," Claude puts in, "it was just a little mouse." He says it like he *is* blaming me.

"No, Claude. It was a great big rat." I look at him so he knows I'm not just referring to that creature that *ran over my leg,* but also to him, the one who turned off the light in the first place.

Claude shakes his head and goes back down to fix the fuse.

Just angry enough at him to get over it—a little—I go back upstairs to wait (again) for Claude.

Though we're sore at each other, we work well as a team. Still it takes us more than three hours to get all of the spider-ridden, crumbling cartons down the stairs. Amanda was right; we both look like we might just have emerged from a hard day's work in a coal mine. She makes us wash our hands several times, then she serves us all dinner, with German chocolate cake and milk after that. Claude greedily gobbles his dessert, but I can't get excited about it. My ankle still feels funny.

Mr. Blackstone tries to pay us, but we refuse to take his money. "You don't owe us a cent, Mr. B.," Claude says, and I agree. "It was Miss Evangeline who asked us to do this. Besides," he pauses and looks from Mr. Blackstone to me, then back to Mr. Blackstone, "I'll be making my own money soon. I got a job. Start tomorrow."

"Splendid, Claude!" Mr. Blackstone says.

"Well, all right," Amanda puts in.

"Yes, sir. Working at Mr. Hershey's store. Every

afternoon and some Saturdays too, if he needs me. Now I can really save for college."

Amanda and Mr. Blackstone congratulate Claude, but I keep quiet, thinking about what he's said. Recently, even more than business, Claude's favorite topic is going away to college. Every conversation with him eventually comes around to "when I go to college, when I go to college." I'm almost sick of hearing it.

Claude continues: "I'll buy a car so that when I graduate from high school, I can just pack everything and drive down to Atlanta myself. That way Mama won't have to pay for a thing. And I can pull onto the campus of Morehouse College in my own ride."

You can see him picturing it, relishing it.

"A fine school," Mr. Blackstone comments.

"Yes, sir. I know they accept only the best students. I figure I have as good a chance as anybody?" The little bit of the question in his voice makes me look up at him. His dark brown eyes are on Mr. Blackstone's clear, light ones.

"You'll get there, son. You got what it takes."

Of course Claude will get what he wants. Who would refuse Claude anything? Except me, who won't let him kiss me and feel me up. So when Claude says he wants to go away to college, who am I to remind him that going away means leaving me?

The sun has dipped into the western clouds and streaked the sky a fiery pink by the time we leave for home. Try as much as I do to keep silent, I end up giving Claude the third degree. "If you're gonna be working so much, when will you study?"

"Late at night. And on Sundays."

"When will you train?" All summer he's been "in training," running at least five miles every day. I run with him sometimes, but Claude's such a pain about training. He works me too hard.

"In the morning, before school." He thinks a moment. "And on Sundays, after I study."

He has an answer for everything. Okay, Claude, answer this: *When will you see me?*

It's great that he'll be able to work and save money. But what about our time together? People started to say we were joined at the hip. Last summer we made a business out of cutting people's lawns together. The winter before that, we shoveled snow. Together. We've watched every Apollo lift-off together. We even kept a scrapbook of each one; well, they're more my scrapbooks, but Claude helped me with the design.

"I think I want to own my own business," Claude is saying. "Be an entrepreneur."

"What happened to being an astronaut?" I'm only half seriously asking, but his answer takes my breath away.

"I'm not going to be an astronaut," he announces. I stop walking. Claude stops too and shrugs his shoulders. "I'm gonna be a businessman, a multimillionaire," he says. He might as well have said he wanted to become a *Tyrannosaurus rex.*

When I can speak, I say, "No, Claude. NASA pilots, remember? We're gonna fly missions together." My voice sounds panicky. I look into Claude's eyes, see the reflection of disbelief stamped on my face.

He tries to soothe me, taking my hand in his. "You'll still do that, Annie. And while you're up there, just know—I'll be waiting for you down here on the ground. Making millions." He laughs and waits for me to laugh along with him. I can't even manage a chuckle.

In spite of Amanda's dinner, my stomach feels suddenly empty. All at once, the sensations that have hit me all afternoon, from the heat to the slimy fur to the blow of Claude's announcement, seem too much for me to handle.

When we reach my house, I mutter, "I'll see you later," and drag myself inside, wondering: How can he change his mind just like that? He promised me we'd fly to the moon—together.

2

My clock radio clicks on at six-thirty A.M., in the middle of the Jackson Five singing "The Love You Save." Great, just what I need to hear after spending all night tossing and turning, thinking about Claude.

He gets a job, so he can't spend time with me. He plans to go to college, which will take him away from me. Now he doesn't want to go to the moon with me. What's next? Get rid of me altogether?

I cast that thought away.

Claude and I have been gung ho over NASA ever since Neil Armstrong and Buzz Aldrin landed on the moon. Every trio of astronauts that have followed them have taken the two of us along with them in spirit. We held our breath through the *Apollo 13* mission and exhaled the same relieved sigh the world felt when those three astronauts returned safely. Watching *Apollo 15* just two months ago, Claude and I marveled as the Lunar

Rover sped across the cratered surface. Now Claude's no longer interested in going to the moon, and I don't know if I can do it without him.

What fun would it be anyway, without Claude?

I get out of bed, shivering a little and anxious to get the day going. Anxious to start eighth grade, get it over with, and move on to Walker High where I can at least see Claude every day in school.

I notice, with horror, the outfit Mama means for me to wear: a wraparound navy skirt with a fake-looking gold pin holding the front flap closed, and a sweater, which wouldn't be so bad except it's expected to get to eighty degrees today. "No way," I exclaim and dive into my closet to find something more appropriate. Five discarded piles later, I decide on my army surplus fatigues and a tie-dyed T-shirt.

"Where do you think you're going in that getup?" Mama regards me with her hands on her hips from the doorway of my bedroom. She scans the clothes on the floor and settles on me looking smug in front of my mirror. "No way you're wearing that to school, Annie."

"Why not?" I complain wearily. Mama and I have fought over every single detail of my first day of eighth grade. She just can't accept that I'm a teenager now and able to decide for myself what I want. Over the past few weeks she's said no, I can't wear my hair in an Afro, no, I can't get my ears pierced. Now it's my school clothes.

"I'm raising a proper young lady, not a gang member."

I roll my eyes. "*Mother*, everybody dresses like this."

"What happened to that nice skirt I set out for you?"

I sigh deeply, knowing I can't explain why that outfit just won't do.

"Change your clothes, Annie."

"Oh, brother!"

"And pick up this mess off the floor."

She frowns. Then, despite it all, she plants a quick kiss on my forehead and leaves for work. Home alone, I consider going on to school as is. I mean, she's gone, and she won't be home until after I get back. Daddy left for work an hour ago, and we'll be lucky if he's home by midnight because he works two jobs: replacing airplane parts at the air force base during the day and driving a cab at night. But, just my luck, one of our neighbors'll spot me leaving for school and say something to Mama like, "What an *interesting* outfit your Annie had on." I don't need that kind of trouble. Sulkily, I change into the skirt, but substitute a plain white blouse for the sweater.

"*Eeuu*, Annie, you look like a Camp Fire girl," Sue says when we meet to walk to school together. She's Claude's sister and my best friend.

"Thank you, Sue, for that fashion commentary." I shrug my shoulders. "Mama made me wear it. She acted like my fatigues made me one of the Daughters of the Black Revolution." We laugh. "Mothers are so out of it."

Well, some mothers. Sue is obviously wearing exactly

what she wants. Painter pants and a fuschia tank top, which matches her lipstick, which matches her nail polish, which matches the hoop earrings swinging from her newly pierced ears. Luckily for Sue, Mrs. Tippet's usually too pressed for time in the morning to worry about what her daughter has on.

On Sycamore Street we join Kathy and Faye. Faye's finishing a glazed doughnut, trying not to get crumbs on her new skirt and blouse, and Kathy's leaning against a fence in sunglasses, thinking she's ultra cool, despite the knee socks and plaid jumper she's wearing. Both of them were clearly dressed by their mothers.

It doesn't bother Sue at all that she is the odd one out. She knows she's cute anyway, no matter what she wears. Two years ago, in sixth grade, she graduated from a training bra to a Cross Your Heart, and right before school started, she straightened her hair and got it cut into a pageboy, vowing never to wear a ponytail again. "The cute boys will pay *no attention* to a girl in a ponytail," Sue proclaimed. Everything Sue does is intended to make boys pay attention.

Sue's always been fast, but now she's simply boy crazy. She has this system for qualifying the cute boys she sees. If he's dark and cute, he's a Fudgsicle. A lighter shade, a Banana Supreme. If he has a good rap, he's a Cool Pop. Tan and ultra smooth, Caramello. Sue says she can get any boy she wants to like her, and she's probably right. She certainly tries often enough. I could be jealous of her except that Mama tells me it's "fruitless" to compare yourself to others. "Somebody's always going to have less or more than you," she instructs. "Be grateful for what you have."

Mothers have to say that. Even if their daughters have boring hair and a chest like a chalkboard.

"So what's the game plan?" Kathy asks as we near the playground of Horace Mann Junior High. She's tall and well-developed, second only to Sue in boy craziness. "Should we hang out and scope the basketball junkies or pig out on chocolate chip cookies in the lunchroom?"

"The cookies," says Faye, who has an insatiable sweet tooth.

"The boys," says Sue.

They look to me for my input. School begins at eight-thirty, but we all agreed to go early today. That is, they agreed because it's the first day and you simply have to have time to socialize before the bell rings. That's not my reason. I signed up to start Mr. Appleberry's Enriched Science class this year, which meets every day forty-five minutes before homeroom.

Mr. Appleberry, an eighth-grade science teacher, is known for being tough on students, and most kids would rather contract bubonic plague than end up in his class. But last year he visited our seventh-grade classes and told us about the new course he planned for this year, Enriched Science. It sounded interesting, so I signed up.

He started this class on his own, without any support

from the school board. He said it's for students who are "gifted with curiosity." You don't have to be an *A* student to take it, just somebody willing to start school early and do extra work. I tried to get Sue to take the class with me, but she told me "no way." Big surprise. Like I said, it sounded like a good idea to me at the time, but now I don't know.

"Neither," I tell them. "Can't. Mr. Appleberry's class. Remember?"

They groan in unison, but keep any further comments to themselves. At school, we go our separate ways: They blend into the throng of returning classmates, comparing clothes, hairstyles, and chest sizes. And I make my way into the building alone.

The door to room 116, the science lab, is ajar. I peek in before I enter. It's nearly empty. Five other people occupy the tall lab chairs, all of them boys. My stomach curls a little, and I draw away. Maybe this wasn't such a great idea. Everybody in there seems like a bona fide square.

I look again. Sure enough, sitting front row center is Michael Greer, the A-number-one egghead of the eighth grade. He's a tall, skinny boy with a big Adam's apple and hair that is so straight and thin, it conforms to the shape of his spoon head. Aside from all that, he's annoying and conceited, thinking he's the smartest person in the whole school, smarter even than some teachers. He's sitting there like he owns the class already.

I close my eyes and lean against the lockers.

Maybe I can just slip back outside. I'll tell Mama Mr. Appleberry decided not to hold the class. No, she'll never believe that. Okay, I'll just make up some story—something convincing, like—

"Good morning, Miss Armstrong."

I jump and blink several times. I hadn't heard him approaching. "Mr. Appleberry?" I stammer. "Hi. I mean, good morning."

"Am I disturbing your morning nap?"

"No, sir. I was just—"

Thinking about cutting your class.

I don't even try to finish the sentence. Mr. Appleberry reaches the door and holds it open for me. I duck my head, murmur a thank you, and go in.

Hastily, I take a seat at a front table, next to Michael. He has the nerve to look surprised. "You're taking *this* class?" he sneers.

"No, I'm here to talk about the Holiday Dance. Isn't this the social club?"

I shut him out with a glare. Michael has never liked me for some reason, and, okay, the feeling is mutual. Who cares if Michael Greer thinks I don't belong in Enriched Science? He probably thinks no one belongs in here but him.

A quick glance around the room identifies the rest of my classmates. There's Sean and Shane McKinney, the twins, best known for their skill on the basketball court. They sit next to the windows, probably thinking they can make their escape to the playground beyond if things get too boring.

Ralph Singleton, whose father is a doctor and whose mother is one of Miss Evangeline's cronies, has the table behind Michael. And sitting toward the back of the room is Isa Woolfolk. His family moved here from Boston right at the end of the school year. He seems shy, doesn't say much. That might be because people teased him about his Yankee accent. Still, I realize seeing him today, he definitely qualifies as one of Sue's Banana Supremes.

Mr. Appleberry deposits a stack of papers on his desk. In his clipped, British-sounding voice he says, "Good morning, gentlemen, Miss Armstrong." He's the only teacher in this school who insists on calling us by our surnames. "Welcome to Enriched Science. I trust you all come here with your eyes open and your minds sharp."

He gives me a quick look over the black-framed glasses that make him look like the chief egghead. He is a little man, thin, nut-brown, and on the short side. But every football player on our team is afraid of coming up against him in a classroom.

"You students have made a commitment," he continues, "one which I hope you will keep your entire lives. This class will show you a new way of regarding your world, help you to see things as a scientist does."

Mr. Appleberry pauses in front of a blackboard. The wall above it is draped with charts: the periodic table, the structure of the atom, the paths of the planets around our sun. Our lab tables, though marred by the scratchings of former students ("Bobby and Olivia, 4-ever"), are neatly equipped with ring stands and racks, burners and tubes. Four shiny black-and-silver microscopes are lined up on a shelf along with beakers, flasks, and safety equipment. We sit, pens poised above our lined notebooks, holding our breath and watching him.

"Science is everything. Look around. Every desk, every chair, every book, every chart, everything you are wearing, indeed, even the cells and organs of your own bodies—are all made up of the same basic elements. We know this because of science."

In unison, we bow our heads to scribble his words onto paper. "Put your pens down," Mr. Appleberry says. "Just for today, I want you to listen, and I want to listen to you. How many of you have thought about science as a lifelong endeavor?"

Michael's hand shoots up.

Our teacher nods. "Mr. Greer?"

"Yes, sir. I've thought about it. I want to be a paleontologist."

I blink my eyes. *A who?* Leave it to that square to want to be something nobody's ever heard of. Michael, sensing my confusion, grins in my face. I lower my eyes.

"Wonderful!" says Mr. A. "Who else?"

"A doctor," Ralph Singleton offers. "Heart surgeon, maybe."

It sounds like he's been trained to say that ever since

he started talking at two years old. Still it's more substantial than my aspirations. Astronaut? Admitting I want to be an astronaut to these people makes me seem like some five-year-old kid: "When I grow up, I want to be an astronaut or a cowboy or an Indian chief. . . ."

Mr. Appleberry looks at the rest of us, waiting to hear what important scientists we plan to become. No one else says a word. I certainly don't. I pull one of those numbers where you try to disappear from the teacher's view. Slouch down in your chair, find something very important to read on your desk, or some speck of lint that you simply must extract from your clothing. Of course, Mr. Appleberry calls my name.

"Um," I begin, in almost a whisper. "A pilot, for NASA. You know. Fly to the moon."

Michael guffaws. Even Mr. Appleberry shows surprise. My face feels suddenly hot. This is precisely why I've quit telling people I want to be an astronaut. I get this kind of reaction. Surprise. Disbelief. *A girl astronaut?*

Mr. Appleberry ignores Michael and walks toward me. "A space traveler?" he says. "That's an extraordinary goal. And an excellent place for us to begin. Did you know, Miss Armstrong, that astronomy was the first science?"

At first I thought he was talking about horoscopes, but then he explains that astronomy is the study of the universe. "Do you like looking at the stars, Miss Armstrong?" I nod. "Imagine, then, that centuries ago, in

25)

ancient Egypt perhaps, a young, curious girl like yourself spent hours gazing into the night sky. She saw the same celestial display, the same moon you see today. She wondered what made it glow. She wondered about the cycle from new to full moon. She too may have dreamed of traveling there. But for her, this was impossible."

He is standing in front of my table now, his brown eyes steady and sure. "You, however, are living in the twentieth century. Miss Armstrong, you *can* go to the moon."

A lump rises in my throat. I feel suddenly proud and also, I don't know—*obligated*. "Yes, sir," is all I can think to say.

"You must all seek to discover your own connections to science, your own areas of interest. Discovery is the essence of science. Discovering something new. Something old. Something that has always been there. Discoveries that move the world forward in monumental ways, like Einstein's theory of relativity, or in minute increments, like the quantum leap of an electron from one orbit to another. If you are a scientist, you are curious about the world. You want to know *why*. *"Felix qui potuit rerum cognoscere causas*, which is Latin for 'Happy is he who has been able to penetrate the causes of things.' "

He makes being curious, which I am, sound thrilling. So—I adjust my attitude. Maybe, in spite of Michael Greer, this class won't be such a bore after all.

3

After school, Sue, Kathy, and Faye go over to Walker to watch the high school football team practice. I start for home alone. It feels strange walking by myself. Usually, if I'm going somewhere, I'm going with Claude. I miss him already, so about halfway home, I change course and head to Mr. Hershey's store.

Claude's behind the counter when I come in, stacking cans on a shelf. Mr. Hershey pays no attention to people entering until they end up at the counter with money. He won't install a bell on his door because he says it would drive him crazy. So I can enter silently and then stand unnoticed behind the potato-chip rack, watching Claude.

Unlike almost all of the other boys I know, Claude doesn't wear an Afro. He keeps his hair cut even and short. In a white button-down shirt and tie, which I think he's glad Mr. Hershey insisted he wear, he looks like somebody who *will* be a millionaire one day. I know I should think that's just dandy, but I still can't get over his dropping out of our space program before it even gets off the launch pad. Or to the launch pad.

Claude is calling out numbers and Mr. Hershey is saying "check" after each one. When they finish, Claude stands up and wipes his hands on his pants. He's just about to start another shelf when two girls come in, one wearing a bright green pantsuit and the other, a small-faced girl in a big Afro, wearing a blue micromini outfit. They both call out, "Hey, Claude!" in teasing voices, then pinch each other and laugh. I can see Claude blush even from here.

The miniskirted girl asks, "Have you made your first million yet, Howard Hughes?" Which makes me wonder, Who is this? And why is Claude laughing along with her? Laughing so easily. Both girls stand in front of the counter, teasing Claude, not even realizing or caring that they've interrupted his work. But Claude doesn't mind; he just keeps looking at them, especially the girl in the miniskirt, laughing and—smiling.

I'm too shocked to move or breathe at first, but then it becomes very important that nobody sees me. I pull back farther into the chips and start backing myself slowly toward the door. Easing it open, keeping my eyes on all four of them, I slip through, rush down the steps, and run all the way home.

Out of breath, and now extremely angry, I slam the front door and fling my book bag against the sofa. Automatically, I turn on the stereo and press the radio button set for WCAO, the one and only soul station in town. DJ Harold M's program usually welcomes me home, his fast talk chasing away the silence of an empty house. With my brother Matty married and living in New York and with Mama and Daddy at work, I have the house to myself for a few hours after school. If I feel like it, I can dance around and sing at the top of my voice, but today, I'd rather throw myself across my bed and wail.

I'm angry at myself for slinking out of the store like that. And I'm fifty-eleven times angrier at Claude. A hole begins to open up and widen inside of me, picturing him standing there grinning. I swallow several times to keep from crying.

Okay, I tell myself, so Claude was smiling at some girls. They're probably classmates at Walker, fifteen-year-olds like he is. Of course, he's got to have some friends. But until today, I thought Claude kept his future plans mainly between him and me and Mr. Blackstone. It never occurred to me before that he would tell them to *another girl*.

Steam hisses from the top of my head. But beneath the anger, I feel a little afraid.

Mama calls promptly at three-thirty. "How was your first day?"

"Okay," I respond.

"Just okay?"

"Fine," I say pointedly. "It was a *doozie*."

Mama takes a deep breath. Her voice gets sharply polite, telling me I'd better watch my tone. "Yes, well, I tell you what. We'll continue this discussion at dinner. Please remember to warm the stew."

I hope she cools off before she gets home. I guess my mouth's gotten me in trouble again. Oh, who cares? It's been a lousy day, the worst first day of school I've ever had.

At four-thirty I put the pot of leftover stew on the stove. Then, with nothing else to do, I call Sue.

She tells me, "You should have seen 'em, Annie. It was a feast. You should have come with us."

"Yeah, maybe I should have," I say unenthusiastically.

"And guess who was there. You'll never guess." She goes on before I have a chance to, not that I'm in the mood for guessing games anyway. "Isa Woolfolk. Remember the boy from Boston?"

I sit up. "Yeah, Sue. He's—"

"A honey! I went over and talked to him. His brother plays on Walker's team, and they're both K-Y-UTE."

"You talked to him?" Leave it to Sue to scoop up all the best-looking guys. But what do I care about Isa anyway? When there's Claude—

"His father's a lawyer and his mother's a principal at Bennett High. I gave him my phone number. I hope he calls. Oh, Annie, you should come to practice with us tomorrow, okay?"

"I don't think so," I reply glumly.

Sue complains, "You're no fun anymore."

That hurts.

Sue and I have been friends all our lives. We were born at the same hospital. We used to play dolls together, and make green apple mud pies. Sue and I have always hung out, even though we're so different. But the things she likes to do now, well, they seem silly to me. I'd never tell Sue that, but it seems silly to chase boys. It makes more sense to me to find that one special boy and stay with him.

But then, what if he leaves?

That's ridiculous thinking, I tell myself. Claude's not going anywhere for three years. And he said he'd wait for me, didn't he? What do I care if some high-school girl comes into the store and flirts with him? Anybody can do that.

"Sue," I cut in to whatever she's saying, because I realize I don't know the first thing about flirting. "How do you flirt with somebody. I mean, what do you do?"

Sue is astonished but doesn't miss a beat. "I'll be right over!" she says.

Ten minutes later the two of us are ensconced in my bedroom, the radio blaring, looking through some issues of *Star Teen* magazine. "Listen to this," she says, and reads: " 'To show a boy you're interested, find some way to touch him. Touch his arm when you say hello. Brush a piece of lint off of his shoulder. Take hold of his wrist when you ask him the time of day.' "

"But what if he doesn't want to be touched?"

"Annie, there is no boy alive who doesn't want to be touched."

I don't question Sue's authority in this area. She reads on. " 'Make eye contact. And smile—' Oh, forget this. Look, Annie, if you're gonna become a first-class flirt, you got to start with yourself. I mean, first of all, you've got to get rid of that ponytail! Will your mother let you get a permanent?"

"No way."

"Why not? She has one." Sue takes my hair out of its ponytail prison and tries to fluff it into a style.

"I'm lucky she doesn't make me wear pigtails."

Sue nods understandingly. "Okay, then let's get your walk together. You know, like this." She demonstrates a hip-swaying gait and I follow behind her. This reduces us to laughter, but we spend the afternoon going over every technique for flirting Sue knows. If flirting is what Claude wants, just wait until he sees me at it.

"Sue?" I begin and then stop. I was going to ask her whether Claude ever talks to her about me, but just then we hear my mother.

"Annie Armstrong. Get down here!"

"Oh, brother," we say in unison. Hastily, Sue scoops up her magazines and we go down the steps. Sue greets Mama, who speaks to her and follows right away with, "Annie will see you tomorrow, Sue," her cue to leave.

"Yes, ma'am," Sue says and gives me a sympathetic look before she scoots out the door. I'm not even sure why I'm in trouble—was the music too loud?—but then I get a whiff of the reason why. Burned stew.

"I'm sorry, Mama."

"You could have burned the house down, girl, and you and Sue down with it. What were you two doing up there?" she asks, flipping my hair back from my face.

"Nothing," I reply. "Just talking about—school."

Mama gives me a look like I'm a potential arsonist and a liar, but she doesn't say anything else. In fact, she spends the rest of the evening too angry to talk to me, and after a dinner of cold sandwiches, she goes straight up to bed.

I follow soon after, glad to put an end to this day.

Much as I dislike running, I agree to jog with Claude in Prospect Park when he calls on Sunday because I realize if I don't, I won't see him at all. And if I don't see him, how will I find out where we stand?

"Breathe, Annie," he commands.

"I *am* breathing."

"Then *run*."

Claude speeds ahead of me, then turns around and canters backward. Showing off. We've run three-fourths of the way around the three-mile track, yet he's hardly broken a sweat. I, on the other hand, am panting like a dehydrated dog. The September air was sweet enough when we started, but now it feels like car exhaust in my lungs. A voice in my head screams for me to slow down, or better yet, just to collapse onto the ground. But Claude keeps yelling for me to run. He looks back at me expectantly, a look which says he's the beacon of truth and light and I'm supposed to press on, dig in, push past my limit just so that I can reach him.

"I can't . . ." I gasp before the very last breath I have is shoved out of my body and my lungs simply close down. All of a sudden, whether it's because I decided it or they just decided themselves, my legs become as loose as rubber bands. Before I can fall flat on my face, Claude grabs me and holds me up.

He gives me his most disappointed frown. "You've got to learn how to breathe."

I want to say, "I think the doctor taught me that when he slapped my behind at birth," but I don't have enough oxygen in my body to speak. So I glare at Claude as best I can, yank my arm away from his supporting grasp, and slump into a slow, sulky walk.

Claude takes advantage of my speechlessness to lecture. "Don't look at me like that. I'm trying to help you."

"You're too hard," I complain when I can talk again.

Claude shakes his head. "Shoot. This is nothing, Annie. If you're going to be an astronaut—" I don't like the skepticism I hear in his voice. He never doubted my ability to become a NASA pilot when *he* also wanted to be one.

"—then you've got to be tough, Annie. Those men at NASA don't want to hear 'I can't.' Where you think they get their astronauts? From the military. Before you get to Cape Kennedy, you got to get through Fort Bliss.

Basic Training, Annie, capital *B*, capital *T*. This is nothing compared to that."

"Yeah, yeah, yeah," I grumble. He's right. NASA astronauts have to be in perfect physical condition.

"Physical training for an hour every morning, Heath told me." Heath, Claude's older brother, dropped out of school and lied about his age to join the army. Now he's fighting in Vietnam somewhere. "Before breakfast," Claude goes on. "Running, push-ups, sit-ups, chin-ups—"

Claude cuts himself off. Chin-ups are a sore point for me. I can't do them. My skinny arms just can't lift me past that bar more than once. I hope this isn't supposed to be a pep talk. Tears sting my eyes just thinking about it, thinking, Well, if I have to do chin-ups to become an astronaut, well, maybe I can't become an astronaut. The thought makes my heart hurt.

I blink tears away, making sure Claude doesn't see them. He starts running again, egging me on. "Come on. You can do it, Annie. A quarter mile to go. Just around this curve is the home stretch."

Ah, the old home stretch. Oh, how I hate the old home stretch. It's the hardest part for me, and I've never completed it. Claude thinks that no matter how exhausted or near death I am, I have to jet down the home stretch or the run wasn't even worth it. He thinks every runner has some special reserve of energy and power that you can just switch on, like turning a fan onto high.

I glare at his long-legged strides and the smirk on his

face. I know what he's up to. He does this to me every time I run with him. He will pull ahead of me, coax me to catch up, pick up his pace and encourage me to keep up, wait until we turn the corner toward the old home stretch, and then take off like a shot so that he can beat me to the finish line and look good for anyone who happens to be watching. I want to trip him, swipe that easy smile right off his face, but I have to catch him first, and that's playing his game. Still, something inside me, some little pilot light, flares up, the heat flushing all the way up to my cheeks. He gets on my nerves sometimes, always challenging, knowing he can win.

"Run, Annie," he commands. "Try to beat me."

I steadfastly refuse to pick up my pace.

"What's wrong," he teases, "you scared?"

"Don't be ridiculous."

Claude slows down enough to let me get level with him. "You're scared. Too scared to even try. You know you can't beat me and you—"

His words fall behind me because I take off running, kicking up gravel as my gym shoes dig into the track. I feel hot all over with—what? Anger? Frustration? I don't know, but all I know is I don't wait to hear the rest of his sentence, and I don't look back to see the expression on his face. All I want to do is run, run like a frightened squirrel, and beat him—*beat him*—to the finish line.

I pump my arms furiously but controlling them like Claude has taught me to do. And, to my amazement, I'm breathing, rhythmically and *easily*, puffing my cheeks in and out in sync with my arms and the strides of my suddenly animated legs. I hear my feet striking the ground. I feel the wind flying past my face. And I hear, coming up behind me fast, Claude's surprised laughter. He's laughing at me, I realize, and it makes me angrier. I pump my arms harder, push my legs to accelerate. Claude's no longer laughing. He's breathing, hard, and he's right behind me. Come on, Annie, I'm saying to myself now. Run, Annie, run!

"You think you can beat me?" Claude puffs out. It makes me mad that he can talk. I can't talk but not because I'm lacking air this time. It's because all my attention, all my energy is focused on the end of the track ahead, four hundred yards, then swiftly three, and I'm still ahead of Claude. But my lungs are beginning to tighten up on me, and my rhythm begins to falter. I keep hoofing it, trying to push ahead, stay ahead.

The little kids who are playing on the slides and swings just to the left of the finish line have spotted us. Cheron, Claude's little sister, and her gang of six-year-olds, the ones hardy enough to keep up with the boot camp Cheron calls play. They cheer us on, Cheron calling to me, "Run, Annie! You can beat him!"

I try not to focus on the screaming mass of kids, especially since Claude has pulled even with me. But not ahead. A hundred yards to go, he's running as hard as I am, and we're even.

I run faster, like a running flame. Claude speeds up, pulls inches ahead. I push to close the gap. My lungs send warning signals, but my feet feel like they're no longer touching the track, like they're a current of wind carrying me along.

You can beat him, Annie, I tell myself. Just don't stop.

A few yards from the end, my heart begins to squeeze up in surprise and panic, but I don't stop. Just a few yards more, I tell myself. Just a few more breaths, a few more strides . . .

Cheron and her friends chant, "Go Annie, go Annie, go Annie, go!" But I can't catch him, and I sail past the chanting line several seconds behind Claude. They cheer me anyway, but their voices quickly fall away behind me because I run several yards more until my legs give out and I fall in the grass, doubled up, screaming for help but not making any sounds. Clutching my stomach, sure that I'm dying, I roll over and over, and settle in a heap. The next thing I know, the kids are clambering over me, patting me on the back. Congratulating me? Or trying to restart my breathing?

I'm dying. I can't cry out. I can't speak. A one-thousand-pound bear sits on my chest, crushing out my young life. Oh, please don't let me die here, I silently plead. Let me live so that I can kill Claude.

He reaches through the shouting kids to pull me away. "Get up, Annie," he commands. "You gotta walk it off." He drags me to the water fountain and holds me up. My head is still reeling, my heart still threatening to pound its way right out of my chest, but I feel triumphant. I didn't beat Claude, but for the first time, I ran all the way down the home stretch, without stopping. And for a while as I ran, I felt wonderful. "I did it! I ran the whole track!"

"Of course you did. And you have my excellent coaching to thank." Then he says, "Ten push-ups, twenty sit-ups. Hit the ground."

"You're crazy." I jerk away from his grasp.

He glares at me, then hunches his shoulders and throws up his hands. "You know what, Annie? You shouldn't start something if you can't finish it."

My face flames. "What're you talking about? I ran the whole daggone track, didn't I? And I almost beat you."

Claude has the nerve to laugh, but it's not a laugh at something funny. It's an "I-told-you-so" bark of triumph. "Almost is not good enough. Now, hit the dirt."

I'm so mad at him I could spit. Not good enough? I stalk away, pass the pine trees, which border the playground, and climb Snow Hill on the side facing the empty baseball diamond. After a moment Claude joins me, stretching out on the ground like he owns the world. I sit down, lean against a tree trunk, and look away from him, dying now to ask him about Miss Miniskirt. Is *she* good enough? But if I bring her up, I'll have to explain why I had slipped out of the store like a coward. We say nothing for a long time.

Cheron and her troops have returned to their play. I watch her lead them up the ladder and down the slide head first. Claude and I usually marvel at how tough she is. But today, I don't want to hear it. Instead, I lift my head toward the trees. Sparrows dart back and forth among the branches, chattering frantically, discussing some urgent matter.

"Wonder what they're talking about?" I say after a while, deciding to try to be pleasant.

Claude picks up a twig and lazily twirls it in his fingers. "Earth to Claude," I add after a moment. "The birds? You think they understand each other?"

Claude throws the twig away. "Leaving, Annie. They're talking about leaving this place. Just like me."

Here we go. I stifle a moan. "How do you know, Claude? You think you know everything, but you don't."

"You asked me," he says.

"Yeah," I return, "but I didn't expect you to know. I was just asking."

Claude sits up on his elbows, furrows his brows, and looks at me. "If you didn't want to know, Annie, why'd you ask? That makes no sense."

"Just drop it, okay?" He shrugs and spreads himself back on the ground. I sit straight up, smoldering.

After a moment he says, "Birds fly south in the winter. It's the natural course of things. Just like I'm going south one day when I go to—"

I don't wait to hear it. I get up to leave. Claude breaks off what he's saying. "Where're you going?" he asks, surprised.

I stare down at him, hoping my look is inscrutable. I'd picked up that word from some novel I'd read, and

I'd been waiting for a time to practice the look. "Home."

"Already?"

"If you're going to go into another 'when I go away to college' story, I'm leaving."

He stands and looks at me like I've turned into a space alien. "What's wrong with you, Annie? You know how important—"

"Don't," I insist, throwing my hands up. "If I hear the word 'college' one more time from you, I'll scream my throat raw. College is three years away for you, Claude, and anyway—"

Here is where I should have stopped and just walked away, angry. But I don't. Instead I become Annie from the Opposite Planet, like a superhero's bizarre opposite twin who looks just like the original but has a streak of evil as wide as the other one has good. This Bizarro Annie invades my body every now and then these days, getting me into trouble. It is she who takes over and spills the rest of my sentence all over Claude's questioning face.

"You may not ever *get* to college. It's very expensive, you know. And that little job you have won't pay one year's tuition. Especially since you know you have to help your mother pay the gas bill and the electric bill and the—"

I finally stop. But like a pistol that's already discharged, it's too late.

For a second he looks at me vacantly. Then his eyes

change, focus and darken, and he wheels around. "Cheron," he barks, "let's go!" To me he says nothing. His silence is as painful as a fist in the face.

My mouth opens, but no words come out. I can't think what to say.

Claude takes Cheron's hand and pulls her roughly to the park's wrought-iron entry gate. She looks back at me and waves. I wave and watch them, rooted to the spot, thinking he'll turn around, he'll turn and wave good-bye at least. I watch until they disappear around the corner, my heart sinking more the farther away they get.

You've blown it now, Annie. You've really blown it, I realize as I make my own sorry way home.

5

A week passes before I can even consider facing Claude. But one morning I decide to catch him before school and find some way to apologize. I watch the Tippets' house from our living room window, glancing every few seconds at the clock in the dining room. Truth is, waiting to go to school with Claude will make me late for Enriched Science. But if I rush and get the apology over, if he accepts and we kiss and make up, well—I won't care that I'm late.

Right on schedule, he bounds out of his house and down their front porch steps, walking on tiptoe like he does sometimes. Unexplainedly, my heart begins to pound and my breath quickens. I hesitate, try to gauge his mood from the distance. Did he consciously avoid looking across the street at our house, or am I just imagining it? Maybe he's still angry. Maybe he won't speak to me. Maybe he's thinking about the girl in the miniskirt, not about "baby" Annie. I chicken out, slump down onto our sofa, and wait for my heart to calm down. I'll ask Sue about him today, *then* go to see him in the store after school.

"Sorry" is the first word out of my mouth to Mr. Appleberry when I slink into class late. Generally, people forgive you when you say it, no matter how much wrong you've done. But Mr. A., I find out, won't play that. "Miss Armstrong, you are twenty minutes late; therefore, you will have detention with me after school to make up the time."

"Yes, sir." I take my seat, a little annoyed about my punishment. It's not like this is a habit.

Michael looks at me as if I'm a convicted felon.

"As I was saying," Mr. Appleberry picks up where I'd interrupted, "I'd like to hear your ideas about your science reports."

My chest tightens. Mr. Appleberry says we're all to complete two science projects this year. "Your first one is to be a five- to ten-page report," he wrote in our handout, "illustrating how some scientific phenomenon or discovery affects our lives." I'm clueless what to write about. And it's due—when?

"Six weeks from today," Mr. Appleberry says, like he read the question right out of my mind. "We will display your work at the parent-teacher conferences in November. I expect first-rate work because you have a lot of time to prepare and all the assistance I can give. Now!" he says, "what have you got in mind?"

e, the first waving palm in the air is from the hael.

riting about the new microprogrammable com-p." He turns to us and I can see he's truly excited about it, whatever it is. "This not only affects our lives," he says, "it's gonna change the way we live."

"Good for you, Michael," I mutter just low enough to be unheard. But gosh, what am I going to say when Mr. Appleberry asks me? Bad enough I was late today; now I'm unprepared. I can just hear Mama when she finds out: "This is not like you, Annie."

Isa speaks up next. "I want to explore solar energy systems. In certain areas, particularly in the West"— Here Isa pauses and holds a magazine for us to see: *Scientific American*, with the words "Energy and Power" emblazoned across the cover—"entire houses are heated by the energy from the sun. It's a renewable energy source. But how practical is it in the colder, less sunny climates back East?"

Bravo, I think, glad somebody is on a par with Michael Greer. Even if I'm not. Also, I'm starting to enjoy the way Isa talks.

I like being in this class, despite Michael. It's only been a few weeks, but I've learned so much already. Mr. Appleberry said our universe is forever changing, expanding. Our own Milky Way galaxy, clusters of billions of stars, is one of a hundred billion galaxies. These huge numbers excite me. I've always liked staring at the stars from my bedroom window, and now I know there are billions more beyond what I can see. Are there people living out there? Is there a girl somewhere, wondering about me? I know the names of the stars, the constellations, and how to predict where they'll turn up from night to night. I think I'd like to study the universe for a living, between trips to the moon.

We do experiments every week, my favorite ones being speed calculations, the same basic science needed to lift a Saturn rocket out of Earth's atmosphere. One day we'll be able to build a rocket to take us beyond the moon, beyond Mars. Beyond the Milky Way?

I think I want to be an astronomer along with being an astronaut. Or an astrophysicist. These are words I never understood before. All I'm learning shows me how much I don't know and makes me wonder whether everybody in here, not just Michael, is smarter than I am.

Lightning cracks across the sky and thunder shakes the air above us. We turn toward the windows and silently watch the storm developing, the fifth in two weeks. Sean, sitting by the windows as usual, observes the growing gloom outside and says, "I got a topic. I want to find out why it's raining so much. *I'm sick of this rain!*"

We laugh together and Mr. Appleberry lets us watch the storm for a while. Then he goes back to the topic of discussion. "Miss Armstrong, what are your plans?"

"I'm still working on my idea," I answer. Sounds better than *I haven't got a clue.*

I walk through classes in a fog all day, my mind jumping from one question to another or going blank altogether. Mrs. Vecchionne, our math teacher, scolds me in front of everybody for being "out to lunch." Embarrassed, I try to keep alert, but it's no use. I wonder about Claude. Will he hate me forever as much as he must hate me now? How could I have said such mean things to him? True things—but mean. I wonder about myself. What's wrong with me that I would be so mean to my friend?

At the end of my detention, which I spend solving all the algebra problems I got wrong on my last test in Mrs. Vecchionne's class, Mr. Appleberry looks at me for a long, uncomfortable moment. I consider trying "I'm sorry" again, but before I can say anything, he reaches into his desk and draws out a sealed envelope. With dread, I realize it's a letter addressed to my parents, probably telling them what a slacker they have for a daughter. Just what I need.

Mr. A. speaks slowly, his pronunciation exact. "I want you and your family to consider carefully the contents of this envelope," he begins.

"What's it about?"

"I've enclosed an application for admission to McAllen High School's magnet program. I'm encouraging everyone in Enriched Science to apply for a spot in next year's freshman class." Mr. A. doesn't notice, or he ignores, my surprised look. "It's the best school in the state for a girl with your talents and ambitions. You'll get a private-school education at a public institution. But I tell you, Miss Armstrong, it won't be easy. The best in the region apply to McAllen. You will be accepted, of course, but it is a rigorous program. If your tardiness today is an indication of your level of commitment, I wonder whether you are ready for this."

"But Mr. Appleberry," I say simply, "I can't go to McAllen."

He blinks at me through the thick panes of his glasses. "Why ever not?"

"Because it's . . ." I swallow. Because it's all the way across town. And I don't know anybody there. I'm going to Walker High School, around the corner and up the street. Everyone I know in high school goes to Madame C. J. Walker High School. Including Claude. Besides, only smart people go to McAllen. Eggheads.

These thoughts rush through my mind, but the only words I manage are, "I just don't—want to."

Even as I say it, it sounds childish and petulant. Mr. A. waves me out the door. "Deliver the letter. The application must be in by December fifth. You and your parents decide."

My parents will go right along with what my teacher says, I think miserably as I leave the building. I won't have any decision except theirs.

Me at McAllen?

My heart actually flutters briefly, a spark of excitement. Annie Armstrong, McAllen High School graduate. McAllen is like the Harvard of high schools around here.

If I want to be a scientist, it's the best school to attend. Even I know that.

Still. No way do I belong there. Not me.

Sue waited for me after school. As usual, a crowd of boys hangs around her. Today, she's holding court with Zeke Kelley and his friends. Ugh, I think. Zeke.

Zeke's a bully from a family of bullies. He has a reputation to uphold. He's bad news from start to finish. He's the one boy even some teachers are afraid of. His real name is Ezekiel, but you'd better not call him that. He's nearly fifteen and still in eighth grade, taller than every boy there and built to play contact sports. He's got small eyes, like a rat's, and when he gets angry, they cross.

Zeke says to Sue, loudly enough for me to hear, "Here comes your egghead friend." Sue turns and laughs and waves me over.

I stop walking. I see red. Like I said, I hate being called names. He called me an egghead? And Sue laughed.

I reel around on the spot and start running the long way home. Sue calls, "Annie?" several times before she follows. I keep running, slowing down just enough for her to catch up.

She gasps for breath. "Annie, what's up with you?" I don't answer, keep running, not even sweating.

"Stop running, okay! Nobody's chasing us!"

I slow down to a good walk, breathing deeply, trying

to keep from shouting. About a block from our street, I tell her, "I heard him."

"Zeke is a fool," she says.

"You laughed."

We're silent again until Sue turns into her yard. "You think I'm an egghead, Sue?"

She shrugs. "Well, no. . . . You're my friend, Annie. I'd never say that." Then she adds, "But you are smart."

I've always made good grades in school, done my homework, helped the teacher sometimes, won awards for scholarship and perfect attendance, and now it all turns out to be certifiable egghead activities. And the irony is, as I'm finding out, I'm not that smart at all.

"Mama's got a new makeup set," Sue offers, changing to her second-favorite topic, "sixteen eye colors, four blushes, two lipsticks, pencils, mascara. The works! Come on over and let me do a makeover on you."

"I have homework," I mumble. Truth is, I'm not in the mood for an afternoon with Sue. I don't even want to ask about Claude now. I begin to wonder, right at that moment, whether Claude *ever* really liked me. Cute boys don't like smart girls; Sue has told me that over and over, and it's taken me this long to realize—she's right. Cute boys like Claude like girls in miniskirts.

I wave 'bye to Sue, but instead of crossing to my own home, I head for the only place in Oakwood I want to be right now. I turn off of our street and start up the hill.

Amanda tells me, "He's got company," and screws up her nose, so I know who's there. "Come on into the kitchen till they leave."

I follow her down the hallway, passing the book-lined study where Mr. Blackstone sits at a long table listening to Miss Evangeline and her ladies explaining—or complaining, it's hard to tell with Miss Evangeline. She's examined every piece of cloth, every pie plate, every scrap of paper from those trunks and boxes and now has everything she needs to prove that the Blackstone mansion was part of the Underground Railroad. She's found pictures, property records, letters and diaries, even a newspaper article from the *North Star* dating to the early 1860's. Now the whole neighborhood is excited about Mr. Blackstone's house.

"Otis Blackstone's grandparents had a vision of what Oakwood would be. They helped seventeen other families to freedom, some of whom settled right here. They built this community, plank by plank, brick by brick, family by family. The Blackstones ran a prosperous construction and finance company, helped a lot of families get a good start in life. There are other historic homes in this neighborhood, but this one is the finest. We've discovered a treasure. And to think, some people believe we should look down upon our slave ancestors." She said this last part with haughty astonishment.

I want to linger and hear what she's saying now (for she's the only one talking), but Amanda nudges me along. She cuts me a piece of sweet potato pie and pours a glass of milk. "Where's Part Two?"

"At work," is all I say.

"How you been, Annie?"

"Awful."

"*Uumph*," she replies, in her "what you children got to complain about?" tone. She doesn't ask for details, and that's good, because I'd rather talk with Mr. Blackstone anyway. Amanda takes good care of him and all that—she keeps the place spotless and makes sure Mr. B. eats regularly—but sometimes I wish she weren't there. I suppose she feels the same about us.

She returns to her ironing and her gospel music.

In here, the house feels almost cozy and, well, normal. Thanks to Amanda. Since she's moved in, Mr. Blackstone's bought all kinds of modern conveniences. A coffee maker, an electric can opener, a vacuum cleaner, even a television. None of these were here the first time

I came into this house two years ago. I remember it was during the *Apollo 11* mission and I had been glued to our TV, so excited. Then excitement came to our own neighborhood when Claude and I, along with his brother and sisters, crept up on the old house we knew only as the Humpbacked Man's house. Up to that time that's the only name we had for Mr. Blackstone, and we thought he was somebody to fear and avoid. Now we know better.

Two years ago I didn't know a lot of things that I know now. Back then, Claude and I were friends, and things seemed happier, easier. Now everything seems to be going wrong.

After a while Miss Evangeline calls out parting noises from the hallway. "Just leave everything to me—er, us. We have the good of the community in mind, don't you doubt it. Well, good day, sir. And thank you once again."

I wait until the door closes behind them. Miss Evangeline is hard to take even on my good days.

Mr. Blackstone is still sitting on one of the hard wooden library chairs. He looks uncomfortable in this room with its bright lamps blazing. He hardly ever comes in here. He hadn't even gotten up to show Miss Evangeline and her committee women to the door. That's unlike him. When he sees me standing in the doorway, he smiles, crinkling more lines into his face. "Annie, come in, sit down," he says, holding his arms out to me. "Tell me what's going on in the world."

I hug him and follow that with a deep sigh. "What's this?" he asks, his eyebrows going up. "That is not the sound of a bright young woman ready to take on the future."

"I know, Mr. Blackstone. That's because my future is nothing but a big empty space, a black hole, a dry sea, a—"

"Whoa! Hold on there!"

I slump into a chair next to his.

"Why so glum?"

"Well—" I begin, and then I don't know where to start. Now that I have someone who will listen to me, I don't know how to explain. "It's everything. It's my life. It's me. It's Claude."

"Ah."

I tell him about our tiff, trying to be honest about how I'd hurt Claude's feelings, meant to hurt him. "It was mean, Mr. B., but it's true. Claude's saved sixty dollars, but you'd think it was sixty million, the plans he has for it. That's all fine and dandy, but college costs a lot more. Right?"

"Yes," Mr. Blackstone replies quietly.

"I was just telling Claude the truth."

Mr. Blackstone nods his head, but he doesn't interrupt me. Now that I've started, it's easier to keep unloading. "Mr. Appleberry expects too much. He wants me to apply to McAllen High School, which is like the hardest school around. It's got a special math and science program, which is a great thing if I want to become a scientist, but I don't know. . . . I'm not that good in math, and maybe I won't even make it. I'm not like Claude, Mr. B. Things don't always come easy for me. Maybe I just don't have what it takes."

Just as I pause for breath, Amanda comes in. She clucks her teeth, tells Mr. Blackstone, "You need to lie down."

Usually, he will bicker with Amanda when she tries to boss him, all the time winking slyly at Claude and me. But today he says, "Yes, niece," and allows her to help him out of his chair.

"I am a little tired, Annie, my dear. I do apologize. Come back tomorrow. We'll talk some more. And Annie—" he pauses before leaving the room, "do me one big favor before you go, will you?"

"Yes, Mr. Blackstone. Anything."

"Leave me a little bit of that dark, empty future of yours. Just put it on the mantle in the parlor. My future's so darn bright and full, I could use some of your doom and gloom to balance it out."

I wait for him to wink, but he keeps a straight face. "Sir?" I ask. Mr. Blackstone smiles, nods, and lets Amanda lead him upstairs.

All the way home, I try to figure that one out.

I wait until after dinner to show Mama the letter. She reads it quickly, smiles at me, and reads it again. "Well!"

I try to think of something to say. If I tell her I don't

want to apply, she'll make sure I do it. We end up on opposite sides of every debate.

"Well," she repeats. "This is something, Annie. Of course, we'll talk this over with your father. But I'm sure he'll agree. Annie, I'm so proud of you."

I get up to clear the table. "Well?" she says, this time a question.

"What?" I answer.

"Excuse me?"

"Ma'am?" I correct. Mama frowns and folds the letter.

"I don't know, Annie. You've been a little strange lately. What's going on with you? You just picked at your food tonight." Her eyes narrow. I hunch my shoulders.

"What does that mean?"

I sigh. "Nothing."

Mama stands up and steps in front of me. "Young lady—" her standard beginning when she's about to lecture me. "What is going on with you, girl?"

I shrug again. "Nothing, I mean—" It's risky, telling her the truth. What is the truth? Do I want to go to McAllen or not? "It's just . . . maybe I won't even get accepted."

"Is that it?" She calms down and reopens Mr. Appleberry's letter. "Well, your teacher feels pretty confident about it. You're a smart girl. You'll do fine."

I'm an egghead, you mean.

"Mr. Appleberry says this is the best program available. I'll talk to your father, okay?"

A lot of good that will do. Daddy will go right along with whatever Mama says, sight unseen, and Mama's gonna agree to whatever a teacher says. So whether I want to or not, Annie Armstrong will be applying for admission to Egghead High.

Will it ever stop raining? I wonder as I sit in math class staring into the dark beyond the school windows. The September storms followed us right into October, a sign that nothing is going to improve in my dismal life. For weeks Claude has not so much as breathed in my direction. He must absolutely hate me now. All because I told him the truth. I could get angry about it if I weren't so sad.

"Hhmmmmmmm," I sigh deeply, unconsciously, and unfortunately, loudly enough to catch Mrs. Vecchionne's attention. Mrs. Vecchionne is small and quick, with black hair and eyes and the faint beginnings of a mustache. She's listed in the Teachers Dictionary under "mean." So my heart lurches to my throat as she approaches me. I glance around the room for aid from someone, anyone, but all I see are averted faces and covered grins. In other words, I know I have it coming, so I brace myself.

"Annie Armstrong. Am I boring you? Because if I am, I do believe you'll find more excitement in the principal's office." Mrs. Vecchionne often asks you a question, not expecting you to answer. She is one lady you simply do not talk back to. We all know that. So I sit quietly, face flaming in embarrassment.

"I can't imagine why this would be the least bit interesting to you. There is no reason in the world why you, a young woman who wants to be a scientist—"

Now how did she know that?

"—would have any interest at all in learning algebra."

I want to learn, I mouth silently. But you make it so hard. Placing letters where numbers should be. Not explaining, just racing on even when I miss something you say because I'm thinking about Claude.

Suddenly, I'm angry instead of embarrassed. How unfair it all is. Everything I want to do is out of my control, and all I can ever do is what teachers, parents, adults tell me. I look into Mrs. Vecchionne's eyes and hold my stare.

I offer no apology and no defense.

"You will stay after school, Annie. Thirty minutes."

I can't help it. It bursts out of me. "Why?"

Mrs. Vecchionne, who had turned around to the front of the room, wheels back to me, fire in those black eyes.

"I mean—" I stammer, "what did I do?"

The room is silent and no one moves for several moments. Mrs. Vecchionne's voice drops down so low I have to strain to hear each word. "I will not tolerate such insolence in my classroom. You will behave like a young lady and a student at all times here. Since you are unable to do that right now, Annie, you may gather your books and take them with you to Mrs. Washington's office."

"I wasn't trying to be *insolent*," I throw her word back at her, "I just asked—" In a few quick steps, she's on the intercom. She speaks sharply to the office secretary. Suddenly feeling tired and forlorn, I start my long walk to the door, my classmates' eyes boring into every pore. I keep my head down, refusing to look at anyone, but I feel Michael's sneer and Isa's frown and the curiosity of the rest of them. What's wrong with Egghead Annie?

"What is wrong with you, girl?" Mama asks as we exit from my dressing-down in Mrs. Washington's office. The school secretary called Mama away from her job to come see about me, and she is none too happy about it. All I keep thinking is I'm glad they didn't call Daddy. Not that he would have come anyway.

"I didn't do anything but sigh," I say for the umpteenth time. I'm tired of trying to explain it. Mama hadn't heard a word I said in my defense. She heard Mrs. Vecchionne's side of the story and believed her, believed that I was being rude and impertinent, whatever that is. I hate being called something that I don't know what it is.

"Well, why are you sighing during math class? You're supposed to be doing math."

I shrug and say nothing.

Mama fills Daddy in on the incident later that night as they sit across from me on the living room sofa. The anger I felt earlier at everybody and everything burns into a hard little rock inside me. There's no use trying to explain anything to them. So I just sit and listen.

"You got to think about what you say to people, Annie, and how you say it. Folks ain't gonna take a lot of backtalk from you. You'll find that more and more as you grow up," Daddy scolds.

"But, Daddy," I begin, "all I said was—"

"It don't matter what you said. It's how you said it. And it's saying anything at all."

I fold my arms and stare silently out of the window. Okay, I'm not supposed to talk. Fine with me.

I say practically nothing to them beyond "yes, ma'am" and "yes, sir" for almost two weeks, until a couple of Saturdays later.

I lie in bed until eleven o'clock Saturday morning, wondering when my mother is going to come hollering up the stairs for me to get out of bed. She doesn't usually allow any of us to sleep this long, even on Saturday. It's a family tradition or something. Even though everybody works all week, Saturday morning we have to get up and work some more. Daddy's cool with that, because he's an early riser every day. He's usually up by seven, bright and cheerful. By one o'clock he's finished all his projects for the day, and he's ready to plant himself to watch sports on television.

I squeeze back under the covers. Maybe I'll just stay here for now. And later, if I can wrest the TV away from my father, I'll catch an old movie. Something romantically sad—to mirror my mood.

But Daddy has other plans. "Annie, get down here!" he calls grumpily from the stairway. I groan. Now what have I done?

On comes my robe. I pad barefoot to the top of the stairs. "Yes, sir?" I say, rubbing my eyes like I've just now awakened.

He squints up at me. "When did I ask you to tie up the newspapers out in the garage?"

I don't answer right away. I remember he gave me that chore two weeks ago, but until he mentioned it just now—I'd forgotten about it.

Before I open my mouth, Daddy answers his own question. "A month ago, Annie." I don't argue the point.

"I'll do it right now," I tell him, turning to go back to my room.

The papers are soggy, but I get them neatly folded and tied with string. I stack them on a shelf, ready now for the next school paper drive.

It's still raining. Thunder rumbles nearby. Maybe I'll hide out here, avoid my parents altogether. Problem is, I'm getting hungry. So I go in.

Mama gives me tomato soup and crackers in one of the big blue bowls, my favorites. They've finished lunch, but Daddy remains at the table, commenting on the news in the paper while I eat. Their conversation skips from subject to subject, thankfully none of them concerning me, until Mama, out of the blue, mentions the parent-teacher conferences in November.

I wince, remembering my latest math test grade—a *C*. The test will be prominent in Mrs. Vecchionne's conference, I'm sure.

"It'd be nice if we *both* go, Slim," Mama says. I concentrate on my soup, sensing a confrontation between the two of them. Daddy has never gone to any parent-teacher conferences. In fact, he's never come to any school functions, not even when I was a daisy in the school play in second grade. Mama says, "I'm sick of being there by myself."

"When is it, Sara?" he asks. She tells him and he shakes his head. "With so much overtime, holidays coming on, I don't know—" He looks at me. "I'll try to make it, Annie. But—"

"It's okay," I offer quickly. "Neither one of you has to go. It's no big deal." I catch Mama's keen expression from the corner of my eye.

"You have something at that school you don't want us to see?" Mama queries. Why does she have to be so suspicious?

"No. Gosh—just drop it," I snap. Mama clamps her mouth shut and glares at Daddy as if to say, "See!" For his part, Daddy puts aside his paper to peer at me. All I can think is, oops!

Luckily, and I mean just at that moment, the telephone rings. I run to the living room and answer it in the middle of its second ring.

"Whassis sisappenin', little sis?"

It's Matty! "Hey," I exclaim, "how's New York?"

"Cool, baby sis, cool. You should be here. In fact, that's why I'm calling. Clarice and I can't make the scene for Thanksgiving, Annie. Gotta work, you know. So, she suggested—well, we both did—that y'all come here. What'cha think?"

What do I think? It's got to be the best idea I've heard all year. Me, in New York City! "Well," I reply breathlessly, "only if you twist my arm."

He laughs. Mama arrives to take the phone. Her whole body breaks into a smile hearing Matty's voice. "Matt, honey. Everything's all right?"

Mama looks happy talking to Matty. She brightens even more when his wife Clarice comes to the phone. I watch her, my hands folded in a prayer, thinking, Keep her that way. Keep her in a good mood.

I've never been anywhere beyond this city except to the zoo in Cincinnati. My mind races to what it must be like in the Big Apple: bright lights, wide avenues, movie stars walking the street just like anybody.

Mama's voice drops a few registers. "I don't know, Clarice." Oh please, let Clarice have asked her the half life of a carbon atom or the meaning of existence—anything my mother won't know except, "Will you come to New York?"

"You know Slim's working a lot these days. I doubt we can take time off." My heart sinks into a black hole. "Annie? By herself?" My heart races up again. Mama hangs up shortly after.

"Can I go? Can I go?"

"Calm down, Annie. We have other business to discuss before there is any talk of a trip to New York." She doesn't easily lose her place. Even though interrupted by a call from her long-lost son, she didn't forget where we were right before he called.

Immediately, I feel sorry for all the sassy lines I've given her, the morose silent treatment, and the lax way I've done my chores. Sorry—because I know all that's going to count against me now. But I'm still irritated that she won't even *talk* about New York.

"Please let me go, Mama. *Please.*"

She leads me back into the kitchen.

Mama doesn't even mention the call before she directs Daddy to "say something to this girl."

"Now, Annie, we just won't have that kind of disrespect around here."

"Yes, sir."

"Don't let me ever hear you use that tone of voice with your mother again."

"Yes, sir."

I try to look like someone with a golden halo over her head, try to banish the Bizarro Annie for good. "I'll clean my room every day. And I'll wash the dishes. I'll stop pestering you about getting my ears pierced. I'll do a thousand math problems—"

Mama interrupts with a hand. "Promises mean nothing, Annie. You've got to change your behavior."

"Then can I—" I begin, but she cuts me off again.

"Let's see some improvement first. We can talk about other things—*later.*"

I get it. Mama doesn't want Daddy to know about Matty and Clarice's invitation yet. With Daddy you have to ease things up on him, especially when it concerns Matty. There's still some uneasiness between my father and my brother about the way they argued and Matty left home two years ago. So Mama has to pick the right time.

Still, "later" sounds like a promise to me. I'm going to New York! *Whoowee!*

Dutifully, I go up and clean my room.

Later on I call Sue. She's the first person I tell about the (possible) trip to New York, hoping she'll pass that on to Claude.

"Sue," I suddenly change the subject to him. "Has Claude said anything about me?"

"Who?"

"Your brother. Claude. Remember?"

"Oh." Sue's voice drops and proceeds no further than that one word. I wait through her silence, not liking the sound of it. Finally, she tells me, "I don't know. You know, mostly what Claude talks about is himself."

I do know. I miss him talking about himself. "Well, tell him about New York, okay?" I ask. Sue agrees, without much enthusiasm.

I don't know what I expect Claude will think about it, but maybe he'll call.

Days pass. He doesn't call.

8

A week before Halloween, Mama wakes me with a gentle shake and a worried look. "Annie, honey. You're not going to school today."

"Why not?" I ask, instantly alert.

Mama hesitates. "It's Mr. Blackstone," she finally says. "He passed away last night in his sleep."

"What?" Something heavy, like water rushing over me, pushes me back in waves onto the bed. I lie there with my eyes open wide, trying to form a picture in my head to understand what Mama is saying.

"I'm sorry, Annie-girl. He's gone—"

"No-oo." The word comes out in a wail, and the next thing I know, I'm curled up in Mama's arms. She holds onto me for a long time, then brushes hair out of my face. "I'm going to see about Amanda. Want to come?"

I nod and, through a fog, wash and dress. It can't be true, I keep repeating. He's there. Sitting in his overstuffed chair, waiting to help me put my life back together.

His words come back to me like an icy fire spreading through my body. My bleak future. Is this what he meant?

I say very little on the way to his house, just nod yes or no when appropriate. Miss Evangeline, looming over everything in a bossy gray-pinstriped suit, swings open the front door before we can ring the bell. "Sara, I'm so glad you're here. Amanda is a wreck. She hadn't even gotten the lights back on. Fuse blew out from that storm last night. Anyway, I took care of that and," her voice drops, for whose benefit I don't know because I can hear her clearly, "I got them to take the body away. Straight to the funeral home. No need for a hospital."

Mama's eyes dart from Miss Evangeline to me. She asks, "Where's Amanda?"

"I can't get a word out of her, Sara. She's in the kitchen. Come on in."

Miss Evangeline had barely said hello to me, but she talks all through the house. "Otis Blackstone was a fine gentleman, respected statewide for his work and the work of his family. It's got to be a fine send-off, Sara. Top drawer all the way."

I glance into the parlor as we pass in the hallway. Every lamp is turned on. Extra chairs from the kitchen wait to prop up consoling visitors. And his chair, pushed against a corner wall.

Amanda leans her head on the kitchen table; her arms

cover her face. She doesn't look up or say anything when we come in. Gingerly, I sit next to her. "Hi, Miss Amanda," I venture, my throat dry. She says nothing, just drums her short fingers against the lace tablecloth as if waiting for someone. I move away from her and go back into the hallway.

Miss Evangeline is on the telephone, a small tablet and pen in hand. "Well, of course I want to look at your top of the line steel models. This has got to be done right, Mr. Brown." Of Brown and Son's Funeral Home. I walk past her, ignoring her sudden interested-in-me look, a look I know means she has something she wants to make me *do*. I return to the parlor.

I turn off all the lamps and pull open the long draperies, fastening them back as Amanda had shown us to do. Bright sunlight, too bright for this day, makes a path across the worn rug. It's also too quiet even for Mr. Blackstone's house, which is usually quiet, except when we come to visit. We could drive Amanda nuts with our racing around from room to room, playing hide and seek, rotten egg, and tuna. Mr. Blackstone never minded. "These children are alive and eager to explore. There ain't nothing they can hurt," he'd told his niece. Grimly, I realize Amanda can now tell us what to do, now that it's her house.

Miss Evangeline lets someone in the front door. I recognize the voices immediately, and my breath catches. Ridiculously, I consider hiding behind the sofa or draperies, but it's too late. Claude appears in the hallway, stops when he sees me. It is the first time we've been face-to-face in weeks. Embarrassed, both of us, we look at each other a few seconds before his three sisters and his mother appear and push him into the room.

Mrs. Tippet hugs me, smelling like lilacs. Even on short notice and for a sad occasion, Mrs. Tippet, who is sharp all the time, has put on makeup and perfume. "How you holding up?" she asks.

I smile weakly and say, "Okay," but the truth is, I'm beginning to feel ill.

Claude barely speaks. Sue, Cheron, and their other sister, Dodie, sit uncomfortably on the kitchen chairs. Nobody says much, watching each other for a clue what we should be doing. Cheron sucks her thumb, and nobody bothers her about it. Even Dodie keeps her mouth shut. Sue nervously swings her legs. I want to speak but find nothing at all worthwhile to say. I want to talk to Claude, but he won't even look at me.

After a while, he gets up and leaves without a word to anyone.

Mrs. Tippet and my mother help the now-sobbing Amanda up the stairs. She looks like a sack of clothes with legs. I run up the stairs behind them and kind of hover around until they get her settled. When I come back downstairs, the other Tippets are gone, but the house is beginning to liven up with church women bearing warm covered dishes, their names written on masking tape affixed to the sides. Someone has turned all the lamps on again. The lights, the women, the whole thing very quickly gives me a headache.

A reporter from the evening newspaper shows up and

talks an hour with Miss Evangeline. She could have
gone on for many more. The way she explained everything to him, you would have thought she'd discovered
Mr. Blackstone, not us. But I'm too sick of it all to care.
Rising from the sofa, I catch Mama rushing from the
front door to the kitchen, ferrying another covered cas-
serole. "Can't we go home?" I ask.

"They need me here, Annie. And I could use your
help." She waves the dish before me. "It's banana pud-
ding, made with vanilla wafers. One of your favorites,"
she says to entice me to stay. The smell of it, and the
pale peaks of meringue almost make me retch. Mama
nearly drops the dish, she's so stunned at my response.
She touches my forehead. "You are sick! I'm taking you
home right now. Evangeline will have to get along without me for a while."

She puts me to bed, sits a glass of fresh water on my
nightstand, and stays until I swallow the bitter aspirins.
I drift to sleep in a cloud of contentment that my mother
is there to nurse me, all thoughts of anyone other than
the two of us in that room pushed even farther away
than my dreams.

I stay in bed for two days with the flu and Mama hovers
over me like I'm a newborn. On the third day, the day
of Mr. Blackstone's funeral, I awake feeling empty and
weak, but better. My head has stopped pounding, and
I'm able to maintain one temperature, though it's "still
a little high," according to Mama. "You don't have to
go, Annie," she tells me. "Everybody would under-

stand." But I insist. I've never been to a funeral before and I'm curious about it. I let my curiosity help me not think about whose funeral it is.

In the kitchen I nibble at tea and toast. "Where's Daddy?" I ask. "Isn't he ready yet?"

Mama finishes her coffee. "He's working, Annie. He can't go to the funeral."

"What?" I exclaim, outraged. "Everybody's going!"

Mama's hand, warm from cupping the coffee mug, touches mine. "It's busy this time of year. You know they hardly let people off for their own family's funerals, let alone someone who was just an acquaintance."

"But this is Mr. Blackstone, not just some acquaintance! Why couldn't he just take one day off from work?" I'm nearly yelling, not expecting any answer to be good enough. I'd read in the paper that the mayor was sending a representative to the funeral. Maybe even television cameras would be there. But not my daddy.

"He never comes to anything," I mumble, loudly enough to vent my frustration but not loudly enough, I hope, to get me in trouble.

Mama answers, "He's trying for a promotion, Annie. It means a raise, and we certainly can use it. He had to go to work."

I push the tea and soggy toast away, sit at the table with my hands folded and my mouth clamped. Mama clears the table around me.

Mr. Blackstone's funeral is at the Union Baptist Church on Corinthian Street. It's a huge church, larger than

Trinity, our church. Mama holds my hand, and anchored like a little sloop to a ship, I follow her through the maze of black cars and black-suited men. The church is packed, almost every space on the red padded pews occupied by old men in old suits and women in big hats. Other men, in gold and black tasseled lodge hats and white gloves, lead people to find empty seats, while the missionary society women, in their crisp white uniforms, hand out folded programs with Mr. Blackstone's picture on the front. I never knew there was a table of contents for funerals.

Mama and I start toward the front, where baskets and wreaths of flowers, white and pink and yellow arrangements, circle the casket and spill down the two end aisles. The casket, silvery blue, as shiny as Miss Evangeline's Cadillac, is open. And there, eyes closed, mouth almost grim from what I can see, lies Mr. Blackstone.

I look away, turn and spot the Tippets in the third row, Claude seated on the end. I nod and they nod back, all except Claude because his head is bent.

Miss Evangeline swishes toward us from a second row pew. She has on a black silk dress, complete with a veil. You would think it was her husband who'd died all over again, the way she carries on. "We've saved seats for you in the family section. Course, there's not much family beyond Amanda. I don't know how I'll get through this. Did you see the television cameras? All the local newspeople are here. He was an important man."

We take our seats. Organ music drifts softly through

the room. I hadn't even noticed it until I sat down and let out a long breath. The organist is a small lady in a purple and gold robe, which matches those worn by the choir, already in place. After a few moments, everyone suddenly hushes as the minister, in a heavy black robe, steps up to the pulpit.

He stands there a moment looking over the gathering. Then he speaks. "Family, friends, and fellow worshipers," he intones in a deep preacher's voice, "let us pray."

Like a great single wave in a sea, we all bow our heads together.

"Heavenly Father, we come here today not only to say good-bye to our brother Otis Blackstone but also to celebrate his life and his legacy. For here was a man rare among men, someone who from his earliest days worked, quietly and diligently, for the betterment of mankind and the glory of You, our Father."

"Amen," a few people put in.

I open my eyes, look to the side where Mama can't see me. The Tippets take up half a pew on the other side of the aisle behind us. Claude's head is still bowed, and I watch him for any sign at all of what he's thinking. Could he come here today and not remember how much fun we'd had at Mr. Blackstone's house? Could he come here today, knowing how much both of us loved him, and still refuse to talk to me? Could he resist admitting, "Annie, I'm sorry we broke up. Let's go together again"?

After the prayer, Claude looks straight ahead.

One after another, people speak about Mr. Blackstone. He had served his country in World War I, as a cook because the U.S. government wouldn't allow "colored" soldiers to fight. He had run his family's business for a time, financing loans, so people could own their own homes. He had served as a deacon in the church, had been in charge of the junior usher board, had met with the mayor and city councilmen from time to time to discuss church or family business. He had taught Sunday school.

I sit there, listening, wondering who they're talking about. Mr. Blackstone was great to us children, but when had he done all those other things? The man these people spoke about seemed to have lived a whole life before I met him. Which, I realize suddenly, he had.

The choir sings, "Let the life that I've lived speak for me," swaying in their purple and gold robes to the heft of the organ and the chords of the piano. Amanda, for her part, remains quiet through the songs and speeches, rocking slightly in her seat every now and then. But, after the song ends, she stands up and slowly ascends the steps to the pulpit.

She has to bend the microphone down to her short, stocky frame. It screeches, but she seems unshaken. She stares out into the church, past all of us, past the stained glass windows, and finally speaks. "Reverend Peterson, ladies and gentlemen of Union Baptist, dear friends and acquaintances of my uncle—"

Everyone says amen. People in church like it when a speaker knows how to address them.

"You have my heartfelt thanks for the love and support you have shown me over the past few days." I hold my breath. She looks ready to crack. "Our family have been members of Union Baptist ever since the church was established eighty years ago. My uncle Otis was only six when he first attended Sunday school here. And I have come here every Sunday since I was an infant child. My parents made sure of that."

People murmur, "Tell it, Sister."

"For the past fifteen or more years, my uncle Otis and me have been the only ones left of this family. And now he's gone." She pauses, swallows, and goes on. "The night my uncle died, you may all remember the way, around ten-thirty that evening, suddenly a strong wind came up. It rattled the tree branches against the windows, and I woke up, startled at first. My windows were all closed, of course, but I could see the branches waving in the wind, for the moon was as bright as a spotlight. I could hear the sound of the wind passing. I felt that wind, not as a draft, but as a warmth—"

"Amen."

"—as an embrace—"

"That's right."

"—a passing touch. A calming touch. A loving touch. I'd like to think that was my uncle Otis's spirit, pausing to say good-bye to me as it left its earthly troubles and cares to return to his Father in heaven."

"Going home to Jesus!" Someone gets excited. I jump at the shout, realizing Amanda is unlocking the gate that holds everybody's emotions at bay.

"I didn't think that at the time, of course. I went back to sleep, untroubled, unworried about anything. Didn't even realize all the power had gone off in our house. And the next morning I woke to find my uncle cold." Amanda pauses a long time, while the people say, "That's okay, girl. You take your time."

When she speaks again, her voice shakes. "You all know I've been taking care of Uncle Otis for these past years, cooking for him, cleaning, keeping him company. But what you don't know is how much he has taken care of me. He was the wisest, most generous, most caring man I ever knew besides my own father, his brother. He's been like a father to me, since my own passed away when I was a little girl. Uncle Otis has always been there for me. And I—" She drops her head, then abruptly looks at us, imploring us. "What will I do without him?"

She sobs into the microphone, and my heart twists up with hers. The minister and two deacons try to lead her away, but she grabs the podium and repeats, "What will I do?" Now, my jaws are tight as I struggle to keep still. People around me dab at their eyes or wail outright. Mama rushes to her, but Amanda throws up her hands, shouting, "Please, God, help me through this time. I know you can help me!"

I'm shivering, feeling feverish again, wanting to be back home with my mother tucking me in, wanting someone to make Amanda stop or to take her away like they do with babies who won't stop crying during the sermon. I sit there feeling abandoned.

Eventually, the organist begins to play, and the leader motions the choir to stand. They sing "Never Alone" as if straight to Amanda.

Still crying, Amanda sings with them. The whole church joins in the chorus. But I can't sing. I don't understand how they can sing. Amanda *is* alone now. She has no family left.

When the song ends and everyone has uttered the heartiest "amens!" the minister bows his head and says again, "Let us pray."

I stay in my seat while the line files past the coffin. I don't want to see him lying stuffed into the satin, face closed and cold. Claude goes up, stands there a full half a minute, not moving, backing up the line. Gosh, I wonder, is he going to lose it too? I remember that this is not Claude's first funeral. His father died when he was nine. I watch him fearfully, wanting to go up and hug him and lead him away from the face that can no longer smile at us. But I can't move. Mrs. Tippet leads him, red-eyed, back to his seat.

Finally, the pallbearers close the lid, sealing Mr. Blackstone away from us forever.

Amanda asks Mama and me (not Miss Evangeline) to ride in the funeral limousine with her. I settle into the cold leather and watch the clouds all the way to the cemetery.

Mr. Blackstone gets a twenty-one-gun salute by his

gravesite in Veterans' Cemetery. Every time the rifles blast, my heart jumps with pain. What a terrible thing to do at a funeral, I think, shoot guns. After one more prayer, the minister closes his Bible and backs away from the coffin. For a horrified few seconds I think they will lower it into the freshly dug grave right in front of us. My knees buckle and Mama has to grab me to keep me from falling. "Just hold on, Annie. It'll be over soon."

I don't want it to be over. I don't want it to be happening at all. I squeeze my eyes shut and lean on my mother. I don't want to say good-bye. I don't want to go back to Oakwood, or his house, and find him gone. I'll probably never go to that big shadow-filled place again because it's empty now, and so am I.

9

Amanda brings all of the leftover food from the funeral to our house that night. On every counter sit pies and cakes, in both ovens are turkeys and hams keeping warm, and on the stove top are pans of greens, mashed potatoes, and gravy. Everybody but me seems to have a great appetite. All I can do is sit there and listen to them go on and on about how if Miss Evangeline gets her way and converts the Blackstone house into a Negro History Museum (she's actually gonna call it that!), Amanda will have to find someplace else to live.

Miss Evangeline claims Mr. Blackstone told her "it would be an honor" to see his house become a museum, which doesn't even sound like him.

"I don't care what the will says," Daddy comments, "if the old man made a verbal agreement with Evangeline, and she has witnesses, which she says she does, that's valid in a court of law."

I wonder which episode of *Perry Mason* he learned that from. I don't like what he said, and I don't like the way he said it. So final. Of course, I keep these thoughts to myself.

"Well," Amanda sighs, "I guess that's that. *She's* got two signed statements from those Oakwood Restoration women. They're all worked up about making the house a historical landmark. *She* says it'll bring prestige into the neighborhood."

"*Sshpt*, prestige," Daddy concludes. "It ain't right to put you out of that house. Evangeline ought to drop the whole matter." But we all know she won't.

I ask to be excused early. My mood has deteriorated and my tolerance level is very low. I spend the rest of the time in my room, making up work I'd missed being absent from school. I start with Enriched Science and read Mr. Appleberry's instructions about our reports. "Use the scientific method. Observe the world around you, your immediate environment. Record what you see. Formulate a hypothesis about the way science touches the lives of people you know. Follow your procedures carefully and test your ideas. Record your results and report what your data reveals. Evaluate your discovery."

I consider trying to describe what's happened to Claude and me as a scientific phenomenon, but it remains a mystery. Realizing that, I can't get excited about anything else. I have no idea what to write about. And the paper's due in two weeks.

———

The next day, Friday, I wake up pleading with Mama to let me stay home. Automatically, she runs her hand over my forehead and, finding no unusual heat, asks me what's wrong.

"Nothing hurts," I admit. "I just feel bad."

She debates, staring at the covers as if they can help her decide. "One more day can't hurt anything," Mama finally says. "But when I come home, Annie, we're working on that McAllen application."

She gives me the once over before she leaves, saying, "I'll call you at noon."

I settle back into the covers and fall asleep. I dream about being outside, in Prospect Park, when suddenly the sky grows very black behind me and the wind picks up, pushing me along. A storm is coming, I know, and I must get out from under the trees in case lightning strikes, but I can't move my legs. I call out, but the wind drowns my voice. I wake up sweating.

An echo of a voice, from my dreams, remains, whispering, "heard the wind . . . power went off . . . found my uncle cold." It's Amanda's voice, speaking at the funeral.

The power went off. Because of the storm. The lightning storm—but why at Mr. Blackstone's house and nowhere else in Oakwood? At least I haven't heard of anyone else's electricity shutting down. Electricity?

I sit up in bed instantly. Grab a notebook out of my schoolbag. Just like that—I have my science report topic.

For the first time in many weeks I feel energetic. I

get out of bed and go pull out the encyclopedia, Volume E. The section on electricity is twenty-one pages long, and includes subtopics like Electrodynamics and Electrostatics, Maxwell's equations and Coulomb's law. Undaunted, I work all afternoon. When Mama comes home and sees me surrounded by what looks to her like some serious schoolwork, she pronounces me fully recovered.

"I do feel better," I say, giving her a great smile. I want to talk about New York.

I follow her upstairs and to her room. She begins removing clip-on earrings, high-heeled pumps, stockings, pulling herself free from her job and settling into home.

"So," I ease onto the subject, "did you and Daddy have a chance to, you know, discuss my trip?"

She doesn't answer right away. There's this silence I've heard before. Which I don't like. Finally, she answers. "It's pretty much out of the question, Annie. You're just a thirteen-year-old girl; you can't travel by yourself. Especially to New York City. There's people bombing buildings in New York. People are crazy in New York."

I can't believe what I'm hearing. But my mind snaps into action very quickly. "If I can't go alone, then why don't you come with me? You can take a vacation, can't you?"

"I took my vacation. Remember when you were sick?"

Sometimes, conversations between my mother and me are like boxing matches. I've just taken a blow to the chest. She had stayed home with me every day; but that was also the time of Mr. Blackstone's funeral. That's surely no vacation.

"Then let me go alone. Matty and Clarice think I can do it. They'll take care of me. Don't you trust your own son to take care of me?"

It's a small jab, but it's enough for her to look up at me.

She says, "Then there's this problem with your mouth here lately."

I stand there like a prisoner pleading for her life. "Mama, I really want to go to New York. I've never been anywhere." My chest begins to fill up. "I've had a rough time—with everything. I just want to get away.

"I'll do everything you say. I won't get into any trouble. I'll find out how much the train costs and how long the ride is. I'll pack everything you tell me to. I'll be polite and courteous—" and on I go, unable to stop talking until I see Mama's expression softening.

By now, she's changed into her pajamas and a robe. It's only six o'clock, but she's dressed for bed. "I'll talk to Slim again. See what he says. Maybe—" I leap over to hug her.

"I said maybe, Annie," she warns.

"Great!"

Maybe is better than no.

Later, after dinner, she pointedly places the application to McAllen before me. "First things first. Read it over,

Annie, and see what all we need to do." I read it without enthusiasm.

It seems ages since Mr. Appleberry dropped the bomb about McAllen on me. Ages since Zeke Kelley confirmed what Mr. Appleberry's news only made me suspect. At Horace Mann Junior High, Annie Armstrong is considered an egghead. A square. An L-7.

I might as well be a leper.

Mama props her portable typewriter on the kitchen table. Humming along, she fills in the blank spaces with my name, our address and phone number, my birthdate. Information about me, but not *me* at all, I think, staring vacantly as she fills the page. When she comes to the big blank sheet at the end, she folds her hands and looks expectantly at me. "This is your part. Your essay. 'Why I Want to Go to McAllen.' " Mama directs me to the chair. "Here you go."

She taught me to type when I was in sixth grade. The last time she timed me, I typed fifty-five words a minute, with only one error. So it would take me less than three minutes to type the 150-word essay they were asking me to write. If I had a clue about what to say.

"I . . . want to think about it first," I say, getting up.

"Annie, haven't you been thinking about it?"

"Sure I have." I quickly add, "But I need more time."

"Annie."

"This has to be really good, right?" I cut Mama off, letting irritation slip into my voice. "I mean—" I amend, "I want to do a good job, so I just need to sit and think about it a while. Okay?"

Mama gives me a level look. But she relents, and I escape upstairs. In my room I close and lock the door, turn on my radio, and fall across the bed. My head hurts again, but I'm tired of taking aspirin. Maybe if I just sleep, the pain will go away. But the clammy memory of my morning dream keeps me awake. I feel even more dread realizing that because of my science topic, I have to go back into Mr. Blackstone's empty house. And worse, into the basement.

I return to school on Monday with no more complaints. In fact, I say little of anything all during the day. It's as if the mechanism inside people that makes them want to talk has broken down in me. It takes great effort for me to even say hello.

Teachers welcome me back and pretend not to notice any change. All day, I quietly take notes, stare out of windows, think about nothing, get up and automatically move to the next class.

"What's wrong with you?" Sue asks, after walking halfway home with me and being unable to spark one conversation. "Why you so down?"

"Maybe it's because I've been sick for a week, and maybe it's because a good friend of mine just died, or maybe it's because I hate being here on this earth—" I snap.

"Geez, Annie. "Don't bite my head off.""

I sigh deeply. "I'm sorry."

"I know what'll cheer you up. Come to my house. Let me do a makeover?"

"Sue, all of life's problems cannot be solved with lipstick."

"No," Sue agrees. "Not lipstick alone. We'll start with a facial and then make you up. Fix your hair different. Just like in *Essence*, how they take those plain girls and make 'em beautiful."

"*Plain?*" I interrupt. "What do you mean plain?"

"Ordinary. They take these ordinary girls and put makeup—"

"You think I'm ordinary?" I ask. I stop walking. An egghead and now ordinary.

"Oh, Annie, everybody's ordinary without makeup. Come on, you gotta see this."

Dodie and Cheron are watching *Clubhouse 22* on TV.

"Did you do your chores?" Sue barks right away.

"Ye-es," they both reply, not taking their eyes off the screen.

"Your homework?"

"Ye-es," they say, before they fall into laughter at something that Malcolm, the host of the TV show, says.

"Did Mama call yet?" Sue asks.

"Yup," Dodie replies. "And she said fix the meat loaf for dinner and make sure Cheron's had her bath before she gets home."

Sue sucks her teeth, unwilling to listen to what Dodie reports even if it *did* come from her mother.

We go to Mrs. Tippet's bedroom. I've been in here before, but every time, I'm amazed all over again. Mrs. Tippet's bed is octagonal, covered in a gold bedspread, with tassels hanging off the end. Her pillows are satiny gold and white, layered so thick I wonder where she puts her head to sleep. Her dresser is covered with colored glass perfume bottles, the kind with a pump and a spray on top of a rubber tube. There must be fifty of them. Jewelry floods out of her satin-lined box. Hair accessories fill another container. The mirror opens out into three angling parts. Sue places me in front of it so that I can stare at the ordinary girl in the glass.

"Now," Sue exhales, like she's got a monumental challenge before her, "let's get started on the new you." She frees my hair from its ponytail holder and crimps it up around my ears. "Will your mother let you get your ears pierced now?"

"She says I'm too young."

Sue huffs. "Well, gosh, Annie. We're teenagers. We're practically grown up." Sue is so impatient to be grown up. I don't think Sue's wanted to be a kid for a long time.

"Well—she lets me wear makeup on special occasions. Sometimes," I offer meekly.

Sue grins mischievously, pulls a gold lipstick case from the zippered part of her book bag. "But I," she brags, "wear mine at school." She reveals the ruby red lipstick inside. "I bought it last week at Hershey's. Couldn't even let Claude see me buying it. Not that he cared. He was so busy talking to Sherry Mills that—"

I pull her hand down from her lips where she'd been smoothing the lip color. "What d'you mean?"

Sue frowns. "What?"

"Who," I whisper, "is Sherry Mills?"

Sue waves her lipstick airily. "Some girl from Walker. Claude's gaga over her. It's a wonder he gets any work done with her always there."

The picture of Claude's eyes gazing into another girl's blazes across my mind. Something bitter rises to my throat and I panic, thinking I'm getting sick again. Sue stops talking, no doubt noticing the green tint to my face.

"I didn't want to tell you, Annie. I told Claude he should tell you, but—" Sue sits down next to me, puts her arms around me. "I'm sorry, Annie. I didn't know you were that crazy about my old brother. Geez, there's so many other boys who like you. Why do you even care about big-headed Claude?"

Her question makes me stop and think. I don't know how to answer her.

She reopens her lipstick. "Come on, Annie. Let me make you up. You'll feel better, I swear. Stop crying, now. You'll make your eyes so red they'll match the lipstick."

Despite my despair, I have to laugh. I take the lipstick tube and turn back to the mirror. "How do I do it?" I demand. "Show me."

Sue grins, reaches into her mother's makeup box and pulls out a crimson pencil. "First you line, then you fill in." She marks my lips with the pencil, then smears the heavy color across my lips. "You've got a nice shape to your lips, Annie. Even without makeup. Now blot."

"There!" Sue stands back, beaming at her creation.

In the mirror, I notice the splash of red lipstick first, then the olive-green drapes over my eyes, and the newly curved and glossy lashes. "Gosh," I gulp, surprised at my own reflection.

Sue pins my hair into a chignon, making me resemble a geisha. "This is what it means to be beautiful."

"Oooh, y'all been in Mama's stuff," Dodie declares when we go back downstairs.

"Mama don't care!" Sue shouts.

"You look pretty, Annie," Cheron puts in.

We continue into the kitchen to start dinner. I check the time. After six o'clock—time enough for my mother to start worrying about where I am. As if reading my thoughts, Sue lights the oven and says, "See if you can stay for dinner." She hands me the phone.

In less than an hour, Claude will come home. My heart pounds as I dial. Maybe, if Claude sees me in makeup, he'll see that I'm no longer a baby. If I'm going to win him back from the clutches of Sherry Mills, I'll have to play the game like the big girls.

Mama asks, "Did you do your homework?"

"Yup," I lie. She lets me stay. I hang up feeling only a twinge of guilt. All is fair in love and war.

Every few minutes I'm checking the time. At six-thirty Mrs. Tippet bustles in. "Glad to be home," she exhales, removing her shoes. "How was everybody's day?"

We set the table and talk. At seven I hear him open the door, and I duck into the kitchen on the pretense of getting the salt and pepper.

"Annie's here," Cheron reports.

Claude replies, "Oh, yeah?" with what I hope is genuine interest. "Where?"

Foolishly, I choose this moment to make a grand entrance. "Right here." I breeze in and place the shakers on the table.

"Hey, Annie," Claude says.

I smile. "Hi, Claude." For too many seconds he says nothing, just stares at the makeup on my face as if it's separate from me, a hat or a scarf that I'd put on. Finally, he exclaims, "What'd you do to your face?"

A few minutes later I make some excuse to go home. "Study for a test," I say, or something lame like that. The point is, I want out of there. I never want to set foot in that house or see Claude again. *What did you do to your face?* What had I expected? That Claude would see me and forget there ever was a Sherry Mills? That he would fall down at my feet and worship me like Anthony did Cleopatra, all because of mascara and lip gloss?

Before Mama can see and comment, I wash the gunk off. "I'm tired," I tell her and take the typewriter to my room. Mama doesn't pursue me, so I don't have to explain why I just want to be left alone.

I turn my radio volume up loud and lock the door. I make a few attempts to describe "Why I Want to Go to McAllen." But nothing makes sense because I don't know why I want to go there or whether I want to go there. Crumpling the sheets one after another, I throw them across the floor. They bounce silently on the carpet. In frustration I fling the pen and notebook after them. Bizarro Annie considers tossing the typewriter, but I convince her not to.

10

Whistle I said before about Mr. Blackstone's house being empty is not the truth. For now, Amanda still lives there. She's shocked when she opens the door and finds me. "I've had all kinds of visitors, people wanting to talk about Uncle Otis. I guess that's what you want too?"

"No, Miss Amanda. I just want to check your fuse box in the basement." I squelch the image of the dark moldy basement and its creepy inhabitants and explain the rest to her. "I'm working on a science report about how science affects everyday life. So I'm checking the electricity in some houses in Oakwood. Making comparisons."

I remind her about the power outage here the night her uncle died. "Nobody else in the neighborhood lost power. I checked with the power company. So I want to know why yours went out."

"Well, I know why. It was Uncle Otis's spirit, saying good-bye."

"Um-hm," I mouth, trying to hide my opinion about that. I suppose it's okay for Amanda to believe that, but I want to check the electrical system anyway. This is an old house. Maybe the wiring is too old to handle a television, a radio, lamps, a coffee maker. I go around the kitchen, pointing out electrical appliances Mr. Blackstone had no use for, but which Amanda does. "If there's something wrong with your electricity, you need to know."

"Go on, Annie, do what you want." Amanda sounds impressed.

There's nothing left but to do it.

I don't like closed-up, dark places.

I've put on life-support gear as carefully planned for this environment as a space suit: rubber-soled boots and dry gloves to protect against shock; long sleeves; long pants, fastened by rubber bands over two pairs of socks, to protect against the touch of slimy fur. For my report I've checked several fuse boxes in our neighborhood, mostly in the newer homes with modern equipment. But Mr. Blackstone's house was built before electricity was available; it was added later. The system it has now must be over fifty years old. And potentially dangerous.

Turning on my flashlight, I take each of the wooden steps carefully. The dank smell hits me about halfway down. I start humming softly, whistling in the dark. I wish Claude were with me.

But he's not, Annie, I tell myself.

Mr. Blackstone's basement runs the width and length of his house. Huge, but not deep; the ceiling is only a foot above my head. Like I said, this house wasn't built for electricity, so there's no light except from my flashlight. And I'm not trying to find anything but the fuse box.

At the bottom of the stairs I scan the far walls. I discover the box in a corner. Humming louder, I cross the floor, lifting up who knows how old dust and leaving imprints of my shoes. The box itself is black metal—not gray like the ones I've seen in other Oakwood homes—obscured behind a spider's web. "Sorry to disturb you," I say, reaching through to open the box. "I do it in the name of science."

I notice right away the rust stains inside the box. Bad sign. That means water is dripping into it from somewhere. The rest is just as I'd predicted. The discovery sets my heart racing, and my breath shortens as though I'd run ten miles. Because this is what I knew I'd find. Based on what I've read; based on what I know about the Blackstone mansion and the times when I've observed the fuses blowing out, I'd formed a hypothesis, followed my procedures, and proven my theory. The scientific method, just as Mr. Appleberry explained it, has worked.

Mr. Blackstone's electrical system consists of only two fuses, four wires within the two circuits with only 120 volts of power and 15 amps each, instead of the 120-240 volts and 60-100 amps all the other houses I've examined have. I do a quick calculation. The total capacity of his system is only 1,800 watts on each circuit, which is about enough to run an iron and a vacuum cleaner at the same time. Not nearly enough to supply all the new appliances. That's why the fuses keep blowing, shutting everything down. If lightning strikes his house, the surge of electricity could be too much for the circuit to handle. It's lucky the whole place hasn't gone up in flames. The long and short of it is, Mr. Blackstone's electrical system is unsafe for modern uses and will no doubt have to be upgraded or replaced.

Writing the paper is a breeze. I start off explaining electricity and electrical currents, then illustrate how power gets to our homes from power stations. I compare Mr. Blackstone's system, installed in 1921, to the one in our house, built in 1961. Two charts show the safe capacity of both houses and the demand being made by electrical appliances. Ten pages, typed, no errors. Four illustrations mounted on poster board complete the project.

Mr. Appleberry registers something between pride and matter-of-fact expectation when he tells me, "Miss Armstrong, good work."

He displays all of our reports in the front hall, a mini science fair during parent-teacher conferences later that week. The six Enriched Science students have to stand next to our displays all evening and answer questions from parents and students about our work. People praise us, and Miss Evangeline (who is there even though she has no children) asks me for a copy of my report. I realize that what I've learned about Mr. Blackstone's house strengthens her case. The place needs major restoration and I'm not sure Amanda can afford it by herself. I thought I was helping Amanda, but my scientific research will no doubt end up kicking her out.

Mama shows up around seven o'clock, without Daddy, with no explanation. After talking with Mrs. Vecchionne, she comes straight back to me. Since there are still people around, she can't say anything, but she gives me enough looks to let me know she is not happy with what Mrs. Vecchionne showed her. Or told her. Finally, as the last person leaves and I start to pack up, she turns to me.

"You've done it again, Annie. Such good work on this project. But if you have a problem in another class, you should tell us that too."

"It's not a problem."

"I'd say a *C* on a major math exam is a problem."

Mr. Appleberry joins us just in time to hear this.

"*Mama*," I whisper, "do you have to tell everybody?"

Mr. Appleberry frowns. "I already know about your performance in math class, Miss Armstrong, and I'm concerned. Mathematics is to science as language is to literature. So you must master it."

Mama smiles widely as she shakes Mr. Appleberry's hand and thanks him, but I say nothing, just continue packing, fuming.

"This was first-rate work here. You must be very proud of your daughter, Mrs. Armstrong. And proud of yourself."

"It's all Annie. We've just raised her."

"Yes, exactly what I mean," he corrects Mama. Then he looks at me. "See you in class, Miss Armstrong. Good evening to both of you."

"You acting mighty sharp around here, little girl," Daddy scolds a few evenings later, his face red with anger. I hadn't taken out the trash, so we missed the pickup.

"Tell you what," Daddy warned. "You keep forgetting things around here—"

"Forgetting what?" I jump in to defend myself.

Mama answers. "Forgetting to do that essay, Annie. The deadline is next month. And a *C* on your math test—"

Not that again, I moan silently. You'd think that *C* stood for criminal.

"Mr. Appleberry told you how important math is to a scientist, and—"

"Who?" Daddy asks.

"Her Enriched Science teacher," Mama replies, irritably. "Randolph Appleberry. The one's been pushing her to go to McAllen. I met him at the parent-teacher conferences last week."

Yes, Daddy, the one you missed. The one everybody else in the neighborhood attended, but you.

Daddy gets back on track. "Your mama and I've talked about this New York City trip. I thought it was a ridiculous idea in the first place, but your mama seemed to think you could handle it. Now—I don't know. I can't see letting you do anything like that. I think you'd better stay right here in Oakwood."

"No!" I exclaim immediately. "Daddy, please!"

"I'm not through—"

I bow my head and bite my lip, forcing myself to remain silent.

Daddy's eyes narrow, and he angles my face toward his. "You'd better pull yourself together, girl."

I nod my head, near tears.

He walks away. I stomp to my room, no longer caring if they yell at me. It's all so unfair. Daddy's hardly ever home, hardly around for anything, but he can cancel my trip just like that.

I pass a miserable afternoon until Mama comes to see me later. She confides to me that the New York trip is still possible—*if*.

"*If* you clean up that attitude. We're still your parents, and we don't allow our children to be rude to us. I know you see that on television and in movies but not in this house."

"Yes, ma'am."

"*If* you keep up with your schoolwork. I know you can do better."

"Yes, ma'am."

She looks skeptical.

"I don't know what's gotten into you, Annie. We've never had to get on you about school. Are you still upset about Mr. Blackstone—"

"I'm okay," I interrupt.

"But this attitude is rotten."

"Yes, ma'am," I agree. "I'm sorry."

"If you're not on that train, Annie," Mama warns, "it'll be your own fault."

It may be a struggle, but I have to be perfect, the ideal daughter for the next week, if I want to get away from them. And if there is only one thing I'm sure about, it's that I want to go as far away from Oakwood as I can.

PART TWO

Imani

11

Seven agonizing days later, after my own silent pleading and public good works, Mama and Daddy finally announce their verdict: "It'll be an early Christmas gift, Annie: a round-trip ticket by train and fifty dollars to spend. You leave the Tuesday before Thanksgiving."

"This is the best, the absolute best—"

"And return on Sunday."

"—most wonderful, most fantastic—"

"*Okay*, Annie—"

"—gift you've ever given me!" I finish and hug them both. I don't know what finally brought them around. But who cares right now? I dance around the house, singing, "I'm going to New York!"

The days until I leave drag on, but my eyes are fixed like radar on the Tuesday before Thanksgiving. I can think about nothing else, not even Claude. Who cares about Claude? I'm out of here.

I'm still light-headed when Sue calls that afternoon. That's why, when she says, "Let me pierce your ears before you go, Annie. So you can be cool in New York," it makes a lot of sense to me. Mind you, Sue's good at this. She might not be able to keep her mind on school-work, but she's a fast learner when she wants to be. Delphine Cole from around the corner pierced Sue's ears, taught her how to do it. Sue practiced on Dodie and Cheron while Mrs. Tippet was at work. Everything turned out just fine, so Sue's made a business out of it, charging five dollars.

"I'll do yours for free," she told me. "Come over the night before you leave."

Monday night, after I finish packing and my parents go to bed, I slip across the street to the Tippet house (hoping I don't run into Claude) to let Sue put holes in my ears.

In her bedroom she makes me hold two ice cubes wrapped in a paper towel around my right earlobe. The melting ice bites and burns, and I get a cold headache. Ignoring my agony, Sue meticulously washes her hands three times in the bathroom and returns with them en-cased in clean towels, holding them aloft like a doctor prepping for brain surgery. Unwrapping her hands, she carefully lays out a size nine sewing needle, a round piece of cork removed from the inside of a Coke bottle top, and several alcohol-soaked cotton balls. These she rubs along the needle's length, and after it is wiped clean, she burns the tip of the needle with a Bic flame.

I whimper. Sue glances at me but keeps to her tasks. "The ice hurts worse than the needle," she says. I'm not consoled.

Finally, she takes the ice away, leaving me with one red, slushy ear. She places the cork behind it and pushes the warm needle through. I flinch as the sharp point pricks, then cruises through skin as thick as a Popsicle. "There," Sue exhales, satisfied with her handiwork. "Didn't feel a thing, did you?"

"I don't know," I manage, holding my stomach. "It still hurts from the ice." Sue dabs away some trickles of blood and maneuvers a silver post earring into the fresh hole. When the left ear is equally raw and poked, she bathes them both with stinging alcohol and sends me home with written instructions as hard to decipher as any doctor's: "Wash every few hrs with alch and turn posts reguly. Keep in fr a week."

"That last part really depends on the person," Sue adds. "It's different for everybody. Basically, you'll know when they're healed. You look cute, Annie. You're gonna fit right in in New York."

I go to bed in bliss, although my ears throb when the icy anesthesia wears off. Now, I have to keep my secret until I return from New York, with healed ears.

Cincinnati's Union Terminal is nearly deserted at four forty-five A.M. Only two employees, identically dressed in navy-blue uniforms, stand guard over the wide empty space, one announcing train departures and arrivals over the loudspeaker, his hollow voice echoing against the tiles, and the other one selling tickets. The only passengers are a thin, nervous-looking man in a business suit—who checks his watch every five minutes—and me. I keep my knit hat pulled long over my ears and stare past the scarred wooden door and the dirty glass window at a sign that reads Passengers Only Beyond This Point.

Every so often, Daddy claps his hands together as if he's going to say something significant, but he doesn't say anything. All three of us are uncomfortably silent, yet I get the feeling they're going to heave a big sigh of relief when I'm gone. Mama taps her feet impatiently, it seems to me, like she can't wait for this whole thing—this send-my-daughter-away thing—to begin.

I understand. I haven't been a peach of a daughter lately. My thirteenth year has been tough on everybody, so far. Sitting here, I begin to feel a little reluctant about going, but maybe that's because I feel ill. My ears hurt. I consider turning to my parents and saying, "Never mind. I think I'll just go home, take a handful of aspirins, and sleep through Thanksgiving."

But that's being a baby, Annie.

The floor beneath us begins to shake, and in the distance bells clang announcing the train's arrival. The shaking floor sends new tremors through me. I sit there like a statue, even after my parents stand up, even after the train announcer says, "Now boarding at Gate C, track 2, train number 50 . . ." The hasty businessman is down the steps before the echoes clear. My parents look back at me expectantly. But I can't move.

"All aboard!" the announcer repeats impatiently. A lump the size of Ohio rises in my throat and the tears spill. Daddy looks at me like I'm turning to stone right before his eyes. Mama, who always knows what's going on with me even if I don't say anything, even if I don't want her to know, says, "You don't have to go. We can do this another time when you're ready." I drop my head and sniff back tears. As excited as I've been about this trip, at this moment I seriously consider forgetting the whole thing. It's scary, leaving them, going alone. My parents hold their breaths.

"Now boarding . . ."

"What's it gonna be, Annie?" Daddy asks gently.

I have to. I have to do it. I have to get on that train. I told too many people I was going. I bragged about it too often. My suitcase is packed. Matty and Clarice are waiting for me at the other end of the 827-mile trip. There is no chickening out now. Unsteadily, I get up and follow my parents to the train.

Mama and Daddy insist on walking me to my seat. Daddy stows the luggage in the rack above me while Mama keeps up a steady stream of reminders: "Be wary of strangers. Wait for Matty on the platform. Don't go wandering around the station. Keep your money in your shoe," she whispers, although there's little chance anyone is listening to her. There are only a few other passengers in this car, and they're asleep. I nod obediently and hug them both tightly before they step off the train. They wave from the platform as the train lurches off. We pick up speed. The lump returns. I try breathing deeply, imagining I'm an Apollo astronaut taking off on a historic mission—the first woman to pilot a rocket to the moon, and all the world supports me and wishes me Godspeed.

A man's voice crackles from the train's speakers: "Ladies and gentlemen, welcome aboard your new Amtrak service." His voice has a note of expectation and excitement in it, and I imagine him sitting at Mission Control. "Now departing Union Terminal for Catlettsburg, Kentucky; Huntington, Charleston, White Sulphur Springs, and Clifton Forge, West Virginia; Manassas and Alexandria, Virginia, and on to the nation's capital, Washington, D.C."

Daddy told me I would have to get on another train in Washington to continue to New York. I try not to panic thinking about all these places I'm going *by myself*, finding the right train to New York from Washington *by myself*, going so far away from home—

I sit back and let the force of gravity press me into the seat.

12

The rhythmic roll of the train quickly lulls me to sleep. When I wake up, the sun shines through the large window next to me, and a man who looks like Louis Armstrong stands above me in the aisle. He has a wide smile and a southern accent. "We're pulling into Huntington, West Virginia. Would you care to go to the dining car for breakfast?"

I don't answer right away because I'm still startled that he's standing there, and I'm trying to remember what Mama told me about breakfast. Noticing my hesitation, he says, "Pardon me, Miss. I should have introduced myself. Name is Carlton Webb. I'm the conductor. I promised your parents I'd look after you. You're Miss Anne Armstrong."

"Yes, sir. Annie."

"Hear you're traveling by yourself?"

I clamp my mouth shut. How does he know all these

things? Who is he *really*? But when I look back at him, I notice his blue uniform and his jangling set of keys, his kind eyes, and his bow tie. So I ask him, "Did you say my parents, um . . ."

"Matthew and Sara Armstrong. They talked to me on the platform before the train took off." I hadn't seen them do that. "All your meals are paid for." I didn't know that either, but right now, my stomach says that's a good idea, so I thank Mr. Webb and follow him, unsteadily, down the aisle. Movement becomes steel on steel sound as we cross the thrilling space between cars. Walking the first two cars, I struggle not to fall into someone's lap, but after that, I get the hang of it.

Five cars back, we reach the dining car, white cloth-covered tables lining both sides of the train, knives and forks and spoons and napkins properly arranged, white coffee cups turned upside down in their saucers, and fake daisies in skinny glass vases. It looks like a ritzy place to me.

Another man in uniform, younger, handsome, and smiling, greets us. When Mr. Webb introduces me, the younger man takes my hand in his. I cover my mouth to suppress a giggle. "Be a real gentlemen to this young lady, Joe," Mr. Webb says in a warning voice. "She's special. You've heard of Princess Anne, right? Well, this is Princess Annie. Take good care of her."

He tips his hat to me and leaves the car. The waiter holds his arm out for me. I take it, and he leads me to a seat. I scoot into the blue bench chair all the way to the window and sit there trying to look sophisticated. Maybe I pulled it off because Joe asks me, "Would you like some coffee, Miss?"

I've never drunk coffee in my life. Only grown-ups drink coffee. That alone compels me to answer, "Yes, sir. Please."

The train pulls out of Huntington's station and slowly builds back up to speed. I watch the open fields swirl past me, broken now and then by frozen, white-tipped woods and an occasional line of hills farther away. I manage to sip the coffee without spilling it, but it's awful. While I'm adding more sugar and cream, Joe returns with my pancake and egg breakfast and a couple whom he proceeds to seat across from me at *my* table.

"Miss Annie Armstrong, I'd like you to meet Mr. and Mrs. Earnshaw." I nod embarrassedly at the husband and wife, two white-haired older travelers.

The woman smiles cordially at me. "It's customary to seat people together in the dining car," she explains. "To make the most use of limited space. Personally, I like the practice. You meet all kinds of people this way." They order coffee. We sip it together.

"It's the worst coffee on earth." Mr. Earnshaw frowns. "But I'm used to it. I understand this is your first rail trip."

"Yes, sir."

"Best way to travel. Been riding the rails since I was a boy. About your age, Annie. Won't take airplanes."

We spend the rest of breakfast talking. Then I start back to my seat, as confident as an adventurer, a world traveler, on my way to New York City on my own. Free to do anything I wish to do, free to be anybody I pretend to be, and no one will know the difference. Hadn't Mr. Webb called me a princess?

The train slows as we circle the Kanawha River Valley. In the distance the colors are muted on the mountains, but right below, the river sparkles like a blue gem. I look down onto the tops of trees and imagine I'm a bird let loose who's now getting her first taste of soaring over the world.

Near dark, the train shoots north toward Washington. Mr. Webb sits down next to me. "You've been a model passenger, Miss Annie. You sure this is your first trip on your own?"

"Yes, sir." I laugh. "But I'll be traveling a lot more in the future."

"That so?" he asks. "Where you going next time? Out West? California?"

"Uh-uh. Farther than that. I'm going to the moon. I want to be a NASA astronaut." Mr. Webb, as I expected, looks surprised. "I know it's unusual for a girl. But that's what I want to do."

He thinks about it. "I declare, Miss Annie, the world is changing." I think he doesn't believe it's changing enough for me to be an astronaut. Still, by the time we exit the train in Washington, and he sees me safely to a new seat in the next train, he seems convinced. "I expect to be reading about you in *Time* magazine one day. I wish you the best. It's wonderful to run into a young person who cares about something, instead of protesting everything."

Not sure what he's talking about, I nevertheless agree.

He tips his hat once more. "Good-bye, Princess Annie."

The darkness and the rolling train put me to sleep before we reach Baltimore. The next thing I know, three hours later, the conductor calls, "This station stop: Penn Station, New York City." My heart does a jump-rope skip. The train slows and finally stops. I'm the first one the porter helps onto the platform. The platform lights are so bright it's like I'm stepping out into a new day.

"I'm here!" I whisper, inhaling my first deep breath of New York City air.

13

People jostle me from all sides. I scan the sea of faces for Matty, feeling like I've been set adrift. Mama told me to wait for him here, but a voice behind me barks, " 'S'cuse me!" and I realize I'm blocking traffic. So I fall in step with the crowd walking toward the up escalator.

It's difficult to move with my heavy suitcase, but I make it to the main level with only a few bangs and bruises. Penn Station is larger and busier than Union Terminal at home. Faces pass me so swiftly, and I don't see Matty anywhere. Matty's never on time. When he started driving and Mama let him ferry me around, I never got anywhere when I was supposed to. I was always fifteen minutes late to the dentist and a half an hour late for the beginning of movies. No telling when he'll get here.

Fighting panic, I look for someplace to go and wait.

Standing next to the escalator is a thin man in a raincoat and unlaced boots. He's clutching yellow slips of paper in his hand. For a second I think maybe he's some kind of on-the-spot traveler's aid, but as I move closer to him, I find myself staring at his face, chocolate brown and unblemished, except that his right eye sits too far off center, almost to the side of his face. I jump when he speaks to me. "Spare change, Miss?" he asks in a watery thin voice.

"No," I gulp, "I mean—" He lifts one of the yellow papers up to me. "Spare change," he repeats pitifully. I nearly stumble over my bag getting away.

I scoot next to a square pillar and brace my back against the wall. I listen to the announcements over the general noise. Trains arriving. Departing. Nothing about a brother looking for his little sister. Take a deep breath, I remind myself, and think.

People walk by alone or in groups, sometimes speaking languages I don't understand, sometimes talking English to no one in particular. I can't help but giggle. This could be fun if I didn't have to worry about Matty.

I start trying to figure out where people are going and why and who will be waiting when they get there. It's a game Sue and I used to play when our mothers would take us downtown on the bus, and we would get to observe strangers going about their day. One French-speaking family holds my interest so long that at first I don't notice the woman pushing a rickety stroller, walking straight toward me.

Truth is, I notice the smell first, strong and stale and sickly. Then I see her and realize immediately there is something amiss. She's too thin, for one thing, and she has on too many clothes at once. Two skirts and about five blouses all buttoned up. Definitely a *Glamour* magazine "Fashion Don't."

I look away, but she speaks to me anyway. "Miss, why cain't I have a dollar to buy my child some milk?" Her voice is whiny, like she's been asking me this question all night and I just won't listen. I glance into the stroller. The baby, under layers of blankets, is immobile.

The woman insists, "Please, Miss. Just a dollar?"

"Oh—Yes, ma'am," I say, fumbling in my coat pocket. A hand grabs mine.

"What's up, little sis?"

I clutch Matty's open arms gratefully. "You found me!"

He looks at the lady. "Yeah, and just in time." He hands her a dollar bill and leads me outside.

Matty's grown one of those small beards called a goatee and let his Afro grow out longer, but basically he still looks and acts like my trip of a brother, making jokes and teasing me as we make our way toward Clarice, standing by a taxi.

I like Clarice. For one thing, she's very pretty. She wears heavy black eyeliner, which makes her look exotic. And her hair is a TWA (teeny, weeny Afro), like an oval picture frame around her small face. She's an artist, right now a student at New York University. And even though she's grown up, she still likes to laugh and have fun.

She hugs me, noticing my ears right away. She also notices me wince as she touches one. "My friend Sue pierced them yesterday," I explain. "They'll be okay in a week."

"I don't know," Clarice says, inspecting them, "they look kinda raw. We'll check them at home. Anyway— you're here! Are you ready to do Manhattan?"

"I'm ready!" I consider throwing my hat into the air like Mary Tyler Moore does on TV, but Matty rushes us into the waiting car.

The cab driver navigates recklessly, jutting in between the packed lanes of bleating vehicles. I ask a thousand questions, gawking at the crowded streets and tall buildings. "Your neck's gonna be sore," Matty warns.

"I'm just so excited," I say, needlessly.

"Well," Matty says, talking to Clarice. "Should we wait to tell her? We can't compete with the streets of New York."

I look at both of them, smiling at each other. "Tell me what?"

Clarice says, "Don't tease your sister. I'll tell you, Annie." She pauses dramatically. "We're going to have a baby."

"A what?" I ask, stunned.

"Annie, you're going to be an aunt," Matty adds.

That shuts me up for a while. I fall against the back seat. Me? Somebody's *aunt*?

Their apartment is a one-bedroom walk-up on West 10th Street in Greenwich Village. "You'll sleep on the pullout bed," Clarice tells me, pointing out their sofa in the living room. Their bedroom is behind a curtain of multicolored beads. Clarice has plants everywhere, hanging from the high ceilings or sitting in pots along the windowsills. As exhausted as I am, once I settle in, I find I can't sleep. Too much excitement, too many thoughts all at once. I just know they'll all cook together in my brain and produce one doozie of a dream tonight. Maybe a nightmare. Matty and Clarice have a cat named T.S., for some musician Matty likes. The cat is asleep on the rug at the foot of my bed, but I wonder what he'll do if in the middle of the night, he's suddenly awakened by my screams of terror.

I push these thoughts aside.

My ears hurt.

Clarice had swabbed my pierced ears with aloe vera gel straight from the plant. She looked worried, but I shrugged it off. "It takes a week," I told her confidently. But the pain keeps me awake until very deep into the night.

Matty works for a department store in midtown Manhattan. After he leaves in the morning, Clarice, who's on Thanksgiving break from her studies at NYU, says,

"It's you and me, babe." She puts on a turtleneck sweater, gauchos, and boots that zip up the side. She looks so hip, especially next to me in my dowdy wool pants and my ugly gray winter coat. Right then, I decide I want to look like Clarice when I grow up.

"Wish I didn't have to wear this old coat and these corny pullover boots," I complain.

Clarice reaches into the hall closet. "Here," she says, handing me a navy-blue jacket, "wear my peacoat. I can't do anything about the boots, but hey, they'll keep you dry."

"Thanks," I exclaim, quickly tossing away my coat for the jacket. "This is cool."

"Now," Clarice says, "first stop, there's a lady I want you to see."

The lady turns out to be the Statue of Liberty. We take the train to Battery Park. It's foggy and breezy there, nearly empty. Besides the man selling hot dogs from a cart and the squirrels and seagulls scavaging for scraps, we pretty much have the place to ourselves. Clarice buys our tickets inside the Castle Clinton fort, and we board the ferry just before it unmoors and starts toward the towering green lady.

A few other people sit behind the closed windows of the first two levels of the boat, but Clarice and I and one other man ride the top. The man wears a beard, fatigue jacket, and cap. He keeps his hands in his pockets, says nothing to us after a quick nod hello.

"People think it's too cold out," Clarice tells me, "but this baby keeps me warm. You okay, Annie?"

"I'm great," I assure her, pushing my face into the breeze, breathing the air, squeezing myself with delight inside my cool peacoat.

As we near the statue, suddenly white rays of sun break through the low clouds and for several minutes she grows clearer as she grows larger, one arm cradling a book, the other lifted toward the gray sky, sun glinting off her torch. Her gaze is steady over the calm water, and I guess if I were coming to this country for the first time, I'd feel safe seeing her there.

I notice a small American flag flapping from one of the spokes of her crown. "Who put that up there?" I ask. Clarice, who'd been looking across the water, turns toward Lady Liberty.

The man with us says, "It's a protest. Vietnam vets against the war. They're barricaded inside—been in there since yesterday."

"Right on, brothers," Clarice shouts, raising her fist. Then she turns to me. "We should support them, Annie, and boycott the Statue."

"Sure," I tell Clarice, but truthfully, I wanted to see if I could climb all the way to the top. The man gets off and gives us the two-finger peace sign.

As we ride away, I try to cover my disappointment. I start to recite the poem about the Statue that I learned in school:

"Give me your tired, your poor, your huddled masses yearning to breathe free—"

"The wretched refuse of your teeming shore," Clarice joins in. We complete the poem together. Clarice chuckles. "I can't believe I remember that thing. I know you wanted to climb to the top, Annie, but don't worry. There's still a lot more of New York to see!"

Our next stop, shopping on Delancy Street. No problem getting people out here. We have to battle for sidewalk space with pushcarts bearing blue jeans and sweaters and people rushing in every direction. We come up to a block lined with tables and racks of *stuff*: jackets, sweaters, pants, hats, gloves, umbrellas, hot dogs, pretzels, chips, watches, necklaces, bracelets, pins, and *earrings*!

"Oh, Clarice. I *have* to get these." Clarice is getting tired of hearing me say that. Still, these are the ones I've decided on after fifteen minutes of changing my mind, a pair of tiny diamond studs.

"Those are real diamonds, Miss," the man selling the earrings promises.

Clarice skeptically inspects the backs. "I have my own money," I remind her.

"You won't be able to wear them for a while. Not until your ears have fully healed."

Before we left the apartment, Clarice had replaced Sue's silver-coated studs with small hoop earrings that she said were hypoallergenic. Whatever that means. I don't care what they are. They're cute.

"If this is what you want—" Clarice says, leaving it up to me. Gladly, I hand the West Indian man one of my twenties.

Elated by my first New York purchase, I'm content

to stay close and enjoy the sights and sounds. People, dressed heavily for winter, had come out and found it warmer than expected. Coats flap open or hang across arms. Hats end up jammed in pockets or on the ground.

For lunch we muscle our way into a booth in a small cafe. Clarice orders French onion soup and lets me taste it. I order a cheeseburger and fries. "Clarice," I say between greasy mouthfuls, "you're so cool. I'm glad you married my brother."

Clarice's smile should be in a Close-Up toothpaste ad. "Well, hey, Annie," she says, "thank you. Your brother made it clear to me I had to pass the Annie-test. He does nothing but brag about his little sister."

"He does?" I ask, very surprised. All I'd ever heard Matty brag about was himself. "Well, that's ridiculous. There's no test. Matty's just trippin'."

Clarice pays the bill. "Anyway," she says as we leave, "I like you too, Annie. I don't have a little sister. Just a younger brother."

"And I've never had a big sister. Just a big brother." We look at each other and laugh and hug each other and go back into the street.

"I just *have* to have these," I tell Clarice in the shoe store on Orchard Street. "Really, this time it's true." I'm wearing the most perfect pair of boots you've ever seen. Soft maroon leather, they can scrunch down around my calves or rise up to my knees and cuff over into a leathery fringe. They're nothing like the boots I'm used to wearing. You don't pull these on over shoes. You don't wear these boots with knee socks. You wear these boots with tights. Or stockings. And miniskirts.

"Fifty-five dollars," the salesman tells me, smiling. "Italian imports." His smile quickly turns to a frown when he sees my crushed look. I have only thirty dollars left.

Clarice says, "Italy, huh?" and takes the boots and scrutinizes them. She puts the boots back in their box, ignoring my stricken look. Then she places the box on the counter and says, "Thirty bucks." She and the salesman go back and forth, finally settling on a price of forty dollars. Clarice pays for the boots and brings them to me. pays for the boots, and brings them to me.

"Here you go, Annie. Our gift to you."

"Really!"

"Yeah, really," the salesman complains, counting the bills in his hand. "From this I make a living?"

The next day I wear my boots all through Thanksgiving dinner (which is Chinese takeout). "Thank you," I say to Clarice and Matty over and over again in honor of the day and my boots.

Clarice turns to me. "Annie. Don't keep thanking us. Thank your parents. It's their money."

Matty groans and Clarice looks at him. "A check came last week along with a letter explaining that this was for food and other expenses of having a guest," Clarice explains. "But they sent way too much. So, you got your boots."

The way my parents always complain about bill payments, how can they afford to send extra money to Matty and Clarice?

My brother sucks his teeth and frowns at Clarice. "I told you to send that money back," he says.

Clarice returns his look. "I am sending it back. By Annie." They both seem annoyed by the topic, so we all let it drop.

After they go to bed, I hunt around for a pen, find it in a drawer, crawl back under the covers to write postcards. I get as far as: "Dear Daddy and Mama. Having the coolest time. Thank you, thank you, thank you. I promise to do better when I come home. Love, Annie"— before I fall asleep.

On Friday Clarice takes me to the Metropolitan Museum of Art. I wear her peacoat, her little gold earrings, and my new boots, so you can't tell I'm not a New Yorker. Except I don't walk as fast. Even pregnant, Clarice beats me to the top of the concrete steps. I'm out of breath by the time we reach the top platform.

Above us a large flapping banner proclaims Art From the Rooftops of Asia, and when we step into the grand hall of the museum, I feel like I could be in Asia. The hall is wide and long and crowded, to my surprise. People sit on the benches surrounding huge rings of plant holders forming a line down the center of the hall. Others crowd the line of desks toward the rear, where you can get things explained to you in French, Spanish, Russian, or Japanese.

The man who checks our coats knows Clarice. "I come here a lot," she explains. "And I still haven't seen it all. We'll start over there."

A great stone building, a tomb like one built in 3300 B.C., stands at the entrance to the Egyptian gallery. I follow Clarice along short, narrow passageways, like a maze leading from one room to another. On the walls, carved hieroglyphics impart some ancient message I can't begin to understand. Clarice leads me to a bust of Hatshepsut. "An Egyptian woman who became pharaoh, leading all of Egypt. You're looking into a world from centuries ago, Annie," Clarice says, "into your past."

This is the first time I've seen Black people as exhibits in a museum. The people on the walls and in papyrus paintings, the figures behind glass, the statues enthroned in great stone chairs all seem to be staring at me. From heavily lined eyes, like Clarice's. I get the feeling they're watching me like *I'm* the exhibit. Expecting me to do something important.

I stare back, searching. Looking for the girl Mr. Appleberry talked about. The curious girl from some ancient time who dreamed of going to the moon. I know it's weird, but I start to think she is here, one of these captured images from long ago, and I want to tell her, "It's possible. I'm going. I'll come back and tell you. I promise."

I tell Clarice what I'm thinking, and she says, "I know just what you mean. Come on. I'll show you my friend."

We climb more steps to the second floor and enter a room with Paintings spelled in simple letters above the entrance. On the walls are giant-size portraits, the ones I expect to see in a museum: overdressed, serious children who look like miniature grown-ups; kings with the look of superiority on their faces. In one of the galleries we finally sit down and I figure Clarice just wants to rest. But she directs my sight to a portrait of a Black man in simple clothes, his hair bushed out into what must have passed for an Afro in 1650. The man in the painting is Juan de Pareja, and the man who painted it was Diego Rodríguez de Silva y Velázquez. Clarice stares for a long time and eventually says, "Check it out, Annie.

"Velázquez's slave, immortalized in paint by the man who owned him. Captured once again. I come here a lot just to talk to him. I have so many questions. I ask him what he thought as he sat there, posing, what his expression means. Sometimes it looks like submission. Sometimes like defiance. And I realize that what I see in him depends on what I feel myself. Do you know what I mean, Annie?"

I nod silently, and we sit there for a long time.

That night Clarice and I meet Matty after work to have dinner in a restaurant on the first floor of the Empire State Building. Then we take the elevator to the highest observation deck, 1,250 feet above the lights of the city.

The cold, the wind, the height silence me. My eyes command the whole twenty-two square miles of Manhattan Island, the Hudson River, the East River, the Statue of Liberty, Brooklyn, Queens, New Jersey to the west. Above it all, the sky rivals the diamond lights from below. I feel like I possess all that I can see and all that is beyond. I feel as tiny as a grain of sand in the Sahara Desert and yet as huge as the universe itself.

I can't explain it. You just have to see it for yourself.

On my last day in New York, Matty takes us on another train, this one uptown to Harlem.

"In its heyday, Annie, Harlem was like the Africa of America, rich with culture. All kinds of Black people lived here. Anybody with talent had to come through Harlem. Ellington, Coltrane, Parker. Writers like Langston Hughes and Countée Cullen. Artists, activists, intellectuals. The Black cultural capital of the nation."

We take Lenox Avenue to 136th Street. Clarice points out a library where the town house of Madame C.J. Walker once stood. "First Black woman to build a business empire. She went from washerwoman to millionaire, selling hair products." I didn't know there was really a Walker behind our Walker High School. Or I suppose I knew there had to be, but I'd never thought much about it. And I certainly didn't know that Madame C.J. Walker High School was named after a Black woman. A *millionaire* Black woman. I wonder if Claude knows.

For dinner we go to Solomon and Portia's brownstone

on Striver's Row. Solomon and Portia are married, and Portia, like Clarice, is an art student at NYU. She and Clarice take me from room to room, so I can see Portia's art collection. Her favorite artist, she says, is Romare Bearden, so many of the framed prints hanging from the walls are his. In the dining room Portia has a painting by Clarice.

It is a picture of people in church, some shouting, some clapping their hands in what looks like pure jubilation. The minister is preaching so hard that he has a handkerchief in his hand to wipe the sweat.

"I call it 'Imani,' " Clarice explains. "That's a Swahili word meaning 'faith.' "

"This is my favorite," I tell her. Clarice smiles and we finish the tour.

After dinner we walk to a small theater close by to see a play about Lorraine Hansberry, the woman who wrote A Raisin in the Sun. The name of this play is To Be Young, Gifted and Black.

The auditorium is small and jam-packed by the time the lights go out. Quickly, the room gets so quiet you can hear yourself breathing, everybody anticipating the beginning of the play. It reminds me of the point in Mr. Blackstone's funeral after the minister said, "Let us pray." Here, though, instead of our heads being bowed, they're lifted, eyes open, watching the darkened stage.

A spotlight appears, lighting a portrait of Miss Hansberry, the same one as in our encyclopedia. She is poised before her typewriter, smiling, her hair curled around her face. She looks pretty and smart and happy. "Ready to take on the future," comes to my mind in Mr. Blackstone's voice. A strange shiver runs through me as the play begins.

"My name is Lorraine Hansberry," an offstage voice says. "I am a writer."

The play shows scenes of events in Miss Hansberry's life. I hang onto every word. Especially one scene in which Lorraine gets a *C* on an essay turned in to Pale Hecate, her high school English teacher:

> *". . . surely you will recognize the third letter of the alphabet . . ." Pale Hecate says in her thick Irish brogue. "Aye, a 'C' it 'tis! You're a bright and clever one now after all, aren't y'lass? And now, my brilliance, would you also be informing us as to what a grade signifies when it is thus put upon the page?"*
>
> *Lorraine answers, "Average."*
>
> *" 'Average.' Yes, yes—and what else in your case, my iridescence? Well then, I'll be tellin' you in fine order. It stands for 'cheat,' my luminous one! For them that will do half when all is called for . . ."*

"It's like she wrote that scene just for me," I tell Clarice back at home, after revealing my own "average" grade in math. I can't stop talking about the play. Clarice sits up with me late into the night and listens. She's like Mr. Blackstone. She thinks what I say is important.

"I feel so bad about that stupid test. Mama was right.

I can do better. But—I don't know—it just seems like, what's the point? You know?"

"No, Annie. Tell me."

I tell her everything and she listens. I tell her about Mr. Appleberry and McAllen. The essay I still haven't written. Mr. Blackstone. Mama and Daddy. Me, turning thirteen. Claude. We talk on that subject until my jaw gives out.

"He's two years older than you, Annie. Sometimes that makes a difference. It's okay if you're not ready to do the things Claude wants you to do. You take your time—don't let anybody rush you.

"Anyway, there must be other boys you like. Boys your own age. Boys with the same interests as you."

Of all the faces of boys I know that cross my mind, only one makes me smile. Isa Woolfolk.

Clarice yawns and helps me to bed, humming the words to the song "To Be Young, Gifted and Black."

"I think you're one of the 'chosen ones,' Annie," she says.

People might think that a strange statement, but I don't because I've heard it before. "Grandmother says I am. Only she says 'God's chosen one.' "

"Bless her heart, that's what she would say." Clarice laughs. "What I mean is, you're one of those people with a clear mission in life."

"I am?" The word "mission" has always thrilled and frightened me. "What is it?"

"Ah, ah, ah. That's for you to discover." Clarice gets up. "I have faith in you, Annie. You'll figure it all out."

14

Mama and Daddy are waiting for me on the platform and they look happy that I'm home. I hope all is forgiven. I'm anxious to show them how much better I've become—how grateful and respectful, how excellent a student, how obedient a daughter, how everything about me is changed. I've traveled alone, watched the world from one hundred stories high. It changes you.

Back home, I'm ready to do penance. Hadn't I been a "cheat," who'd done "half when *all* is called for!"

"*. . . for them that will slip and slide through life at the edge of their minds, never once pushing into the interior to see what wonders are hiding there—content to drift along on whatever gets them by,* cheating *themselves,* cheating *the world,* cheating *Nature! That is what the 'C' means, my dear child—my pet—my laziest* Queen of the Ethiopes!"

Pale Hecate's words—the whole play—are mine to keep forever. Clarice spent the rest of the "expense" money on books. Books about the Statue of Liberty, about the ancient Egyptians, about Madame C.J. Walker, and a copy of the play *To Be Young, Gifted and Black*. I read it twice on the train. In between, writing so passionately that my fingers hurt afterward, I finished my essay, "Why I Want to Go to McAllen."

One Giant Leap for Annie Armstrong

Two years ago the whole world watched as Neil Armstrong became the first human being to walk on the moon. He described it as a "giant leap" for mankind. Ever since I watched that event, and long before, I have wanted to become an astronaut, fly a rocket to the moon, collect rocks and sand on its surface, and bring new knowledge back to Earth. Thanks to my science teacher, Mr. Randolph Appleberry, I know how important it is to prepare myself through science to reach my goals. He has taught me that science is learning by discovery. He has taught me how to use the scientific method to investigate and solve problems. He has made me want to know more, and he has made my desire to take that giant leap even stronger.

Studying math and science in McAllen's magnet program is one step toward reaching my goals. Deciding to apply to your school is also a giant leap for me. It means leaving my neighborhood school and my friends and working very hard, but I'm willing to do that. I would very much like to attend McAllen High School next year.

I think it's okay, but Mama and Daddy want to give it a Pulitzer prize.

"I wouldn't change a word," Daddy beams.

Mama offers, "I'll type it at work tomorrow, Annie, on my Selectric. Make it look really nice."

They kiss me and go off to bed in a cheerful glow. Even though it's corny to feel this way, I can't help being happy to see them pleased with my essay. But is it good enough for McAllen?

I unpack and change into warm pajamas. I jump into bed, snuggling under the covers, but I'm nowhere near sleepy. My mind replays every second of my trip and pretty soon, I'm just bursting to talk to someone. I get out of bed, close my door, and look out my front window, directly facing Claude's room. It's twelve o'clock, and his light is the only one on. He's no doubt studying, or maybe he's having a brainstorm about his plans—or thinking about me.

He's probably studying.

I sit still and watch his window, waiting to feel sad and angry, but it doesn't come.

Instead, contented and eager to get back to school, I go to bed.

All my good intentions get derailed when I wake up the next morning with a set of Dumbo ears.

It's been a week since Sue pierced my ears, and they hurt now more than ever. They itch painfully. Every day it takes more alcohol to wipe away the crust that forms overnight between the hole and the earring post. Mama and Daddy still haven't noticed, but today, Daddy hears my faint moaning from the hallway. "Annie, what's wrong?" he asks, flipping on my light.

He sees them right away. "My God, Annie, what's wrong with your ears?"

"They hurt," I whimper, holding my head.

Daddy calls Mama in a voice that brings her rushing to the room. "Sara, when did you let this girl get her ears pierced?"

Now, I know that whenever Daddy says, "this girl," I'm in trouble. If I'm "this girl," then he's not claiming me, which means he's really mad. I brace myself for a tirade.

Mama eyes me shrewdly and opens her mouth only slightly to ask, "Who did this?"

I tell them Sue.

"Who?" they say in unison, Mama in disbelief and Daddy, for a second, not even recognizing who I mean. I start to explain but get stuck. "I . . . I . . . I . . ."

It doesn't matter. Within seconds a whirlwind of words fly around me and nobody's listening to what I have to say. "I don't believe you did this. Sara, how come you let this girl just do as she pleases?"

"She has a father too, Slim. Maybe you'll take some responsibility now for raising this child too."

"Meaning what? You saying I don't take care of my child?"

"I'm saying you're hardly around to—"

"Don't I work myself nearly to death trying to make sure this child gets to eat, has clothes on her back!"

"She needs you here with her. Not just working for her."

"Just working? *Just* working. So maybe you want me to quit my job and lie around the house drinking beer all day, flipping the TV channels. Would that make you happy? And, Annie, you—" Daddy suddenly remembers I'm the start of all of this. "You pay no mind to what we say. Now your mother has to take time off from her job to take you to the doctor."

"Why can't you take time off? I *always* take time off," Mama puts in. They argue about this until Mama looks at me and says quietly, "Slim, the girl's in pain."

She wins. She gets to ask for the morning off to deliver me to Dr. Shoecraft. He examines my beet-red ears, removes the earrings, and whistles. "I could drive a truck through these holes!"

I've cried so much already today that I don't have the energy to laugh. My infected ears feel like two hot stones weighing my head down.

Dr. Shoecraft gives me a shot of penicillin and seems surprised that I don't need or want a lollipop after. He makes some remark about bringing me into this world and time flying before he sends us on our way. Mama, despite my feeble protests, makes me go to school with my obnoxious ears. This, I realize, is only the beginning of my pierced ear punishment. I get to be on display at school as the girl with swollen lobes whose parents made her unpierce her ears.

Walking home, Sue apologizes over and over. "I don't understand what happened, Annie." I finally tell her it's not her fault, that I should have taken better care of them. "Better yet, I shouldn't have gotten them pierced in the first place," I admit. As a peace offering, I give her the earrings I'd bought in New York. Sue is fine after that.

December grows like a glacier, and I feel more and more like a caterpillar in her cocoon who's not even looking forward to emerging in the spring as a butterfly. My daily routine is school, home, homework, bed—broken only by the television and the welcome excursions into my books. Whenever I can, I escape to the library and load up on novels, as many as I can carry at one time. My favorites right now are Edward Eager's books. I read *Magic or Not?* and imagine I'm free of my own problems. Instead I'm figuring out whether Lydia's grandmother is really a witch and whether there are ghosts in the house in the woods. Unlike me, the children in books have *mysteries* to solve, not problems.

At school I'm all work, enthusiastically turning in essays, reports, and extra credit assignments like a student machine. My teachers have nothing but praise. Mrs. Vecchionne seems willing to forgive my outburst earlier in the semester, although she can't help warning me,

"Your test scores haven't caught up with your efforts yet, Annie. Starting next week, I'll offer tutoring after school for two days a week. I expect to see you there."

True to her word, she holds math tutorials, which can go on for *two hours*, and I faithfully attend because I know I need it. I don't mind, really. For one thing, I'm understanding the problems. For another thing, I'm not the only student attending the tutorials. Isa comes too.

We work very seriously, side by side, on those afternoons after school. It's heaven sitting next to him, so I haven't missed a session. He doesn't know it, but Isa's part of the reason my math grades are improving.

Not enough, though, for me to avoid a *C* on my first report card. Whose bright idea is it to hand out report cards right before Christmas break anyway? It definitely put a damper on our festivities, standing out among my other grades like an ugly ornament on a tree.

"I thought we got this all straightened out," Daddy says wearily. I stamp down the little flame of annoyance inside me. Why doesn't he say anything about all the good grades I got? Why is it he only notices me when I do something wrong?

To my surprise, Daddy lets out a deep sigh, just like one of mine, and I'm instantly penitent. *I'm sorry I've disappointed you*, I want to say. It sounds so lame.

I go through the motions of Christmas dinner at my grandparents' house, visits to friends in town, calls to relatives in other cities. But my heart is not in it. I spend most of the days reading in my room, watching the snow fall and the ice harden everything. When the old year passes into the new, I make a resolution: "I won't ever disappoint him again." But everyone knows how easy New Year's resolutions are to make, how difficult to keep.

I n early January a letter arrives from McAllen High School.

Dear Mr. and Mrs. Armstrong:
(No, it was not addressed to me, but I opened it because I knew it was *about* me.)

The admissions committee of McAllen High School has reviewed your daughter's application to the Math and Science Magnet Program. We are impressed with Anne's scholastic records, and we would like her to advance to the next stage in the process, the personal interview.

I have tentatively arranged an interview date of Monday, January 10, at 11:00 A.M. I do hope this is convenient for you. Please confirm this appointment by calling the school between the hours of 8:00 A.M. and 4:00 P.M.

I look forward to hearing from you.

Sincerely,

George E. Stokes, Principal

"They want me!" I scream.

An interview! The thought both scares and excites me. I imagine standing before three old men in robes having to answer algebra questions. But even that scary image can't keep me from thanking my lucky stars as I dance around the house all afternoon.

I carefully refold the letter and tuck it in between the other pieces of mail so that when Mama comes home, she can discover it for herself and get as much of a thrill as I have.

But she comes home from work with a headache and goes straight to bed, not even glancing at the mail. Mama dislikes winter because she hates getting home after dark. She says she starts getting sleepy at four-thirty in the afternoon. I consider telling her about the interview, but I simply give her a glass of water and aspirins and let her alone. Anyway, Daddy is who I need to see.

I want him to go with me to McAllen. Mama's right. It's not fair that she's always skipping work to take care of me. Besides, with Daddy along, everything's sure to work out all right.

I wait past midnight. He clumps in, breathing fog from the cold outside, and spots me at the kitchen table, munching a snack of graham crackers. Before he says hello, before I can welcome him home, he snaps, "What're you doing up so late, girl?"

His tone stuns me. I open my mouth to say, "Waiting for you," but no words come out. What is he angry about now? What have I done?

Suddenly, it seems silly even to ask him. Daddy never takes time off for me. I'd have to be on my way to the guillotine for him to miss a day of work.

With the barest "good night," I go up to my room, stopping only to tuck the letter between the books in my bag. Who needs him anyway, I think. I'm not a baby.

Neither one of them has to take time from precious work. It's not that important. They don't even need to know I have an interview. I've been all the way to New York by myself. I can do this on my own.

To get to McAllen on the bus, I find out from the Mass Transit Administration information line, I have to take number 88 on Carter Avenue and ride it downtown to Main, where I transfer to number 17 going north. If I leave home by 9:30, I'll reach my stop by 10:35. Plenty of time for my interview at 11:00.

I try to look nonchalant for any neighbors who might wonder why I'm leaving home so late for school. All I need is for one of them to remark to my parents that they saw me on the street "way after school had started." But I don't feel guilty about going on my own. After all, I'm doing both of my parents a favor. So what if I have to deceive them to do it.

Freezing rain layers ice over roads, sidewalks, and lawns and makes getting anywhere by any means treacherous. I wear my new boots, slipping and almost falling two times before I arrive at the bus stop. Two other people huddle next to each other beside me, a young couple who remind me of Matty and Clarice. They tell me they are premed students at Loyola College downtown. We blow smoke back and forth to each other, talking to keep warm. I tell them about my interview. Eventually the bus inches its way to a stop before us.

"Look them straight in the eyes when you answer their questions," the man, Todd, tells me.

"And take your time answering," his girlfriend Sheila puts in.

"You're going to be doctors?" I ask, changing the topic from my interview, sorry now that I said anything. They're trying to give me confidence, but they're making me more nervous. After we all get off downtown, Todd gives me some final instructions. "Be strong, little sister."

They both give me the fist up sign and go on their way.

Downtown streets have been cleared and salted, but there's nothing city workers can do to brighten the gray skies overhead or warm the heavy, wet, cold air or dry the sodden cement sidewalks. People rush from taxis and buses into buildings, trying to shorten their stay outside. Others fight for parking spaces in slow-moving cars. Some kids only a little older than me, uniformed girls in clusters, head for the Catholic high school; boys in different uniforms get off another bus. Watching them hustle along, laughing easily with each other, I imagine myself in their place next year, a book bag slung over my back, going off to a school I have to ride the bus to get to. Two buses.

The second bus is nearly empty, leaving downtown for Cornell Heights. Several women, day workers, sit talking in the rear seats. The three of them and I are the only Black people on the bus. I take a seat near them.

"Shouldn't you be in school, chile?" one asks me.

"No, ma'am," I answer, a little flustered. "I mean, yes. But I have an interview today at McAllen High School. I may go there next year."

"Oh," the three of them say in unison, sitting back in their seats, smiling.

"Well, that's right nice," the first one says. "You just relax now. We'll tell you when we get to your stop."

I try to relax, listening to the women's gossip. But by now I'm officially, fully blown scared out of my wits. As the bus travels farther north, the streets become quieter, the houses sit farther back from the road, and the lawns spread out in larger parcels of manicured land, I find myself thinking, I could just stay here, on the bus. Ride it all the way out and ride it all the way back downtown. Go back home. I could call them, pretend I'm my mother, and say, "My daughter has the flu and will, by the way, be unable to attend your high school next year." They've never heard my mother's voice. I could forget the whole thing.

Aloud, I tell myself, "Don't be a baby, Annie." So I get off the bus at my stop.

To distract myself, I hum "To Be Young, Gifted and Black" all the way up to the front steps of McAllen High School. Carved into the stone arch above the school's white doors are the words *PLVS VLTRA*. I puzzle over this until I realize the words are Latin and what looks like *V*'s are read as *U*'s. *"Plus ultra,"* I mouth. Now what does that mean?

Inside, straight ahead, a wall of glass trophy cases spreads along the hallway. Over the sixty years of the school's existence, McAllen's students have carried home rows of silver and gold honors. I read some of the names and dates on the trophies as I continue to the office and sign my name in the Visitors' book.

The principal's secretary shows me to a chair in his waiting room. She introduces me to another interviewee there, a boy named Solon Wainwright, and his parents. "You're next," she tells me when the Wainwrights go into the principal's office. "Good-bye, Charles, Mr. and Mrs. Smith," she calls to the people who've just come out. I realize miserably that everyone else is traveling in threesomes, and I'm all alone.

I could walk out. I could pretend I'm suddenly ill, or I suddenly remembered an important test at school that I just can't miss, so maybe we'd better forget about this McAllen business after all.

I take in a few deep breaths and force myself to stay.

The Wainwrights reemerge from the office, wave a satisfied good-bye, and ignore me when they leave. A tall man, the principal, greets me and waves me in. My heart lurches, but I manage to walk into his office. He closes the door and motions me to a seat.

"Good morning, Miss Armstrong. I'm Mr. Stokes." He nods to the two other people sitting in chairs behind a table in front of me. "This is Mrs. Biery and Mr. Klein." I say hello, my voice betraying me with a quiver, and look each one in the eye. Then Mr. Stokes asks the first question.

"Tell us a little about yourself, Anne." As if struck by lightning, I sit there unable to speak or think clearly for several seconds. A simple question, but I don't know where to start. What is "a little about myself"? There's so much I could tell. And yet there's so very little I'm sure about that maybe I can't say anything that makes sense. Stuttering, I start. "I am thirteen years old, in the eighth grade at Horace Mann Junior High." Of course, they know all of that, I think, but I keep going, thinking, Okay, you've covered "young," now do "gifted." I keep my eyes on their eyes, shifting from Mr. Stokes to Mrs. Biery to Mr. Klein. "I like school, I get good grades, and . . ." I consider this next part before I say it, and so it comes out stronger than the previous information had, ". . . and I want to go to college, study astronomy, and eventually become an astronaut and fly a mission to the moon."

I watch their faces for the look—the look that says "a girl astronaut?" They make small nods and write on their forms. A good sign. I exhale again.

Before I can get too comfortable, Mrs. Biery stuns me with her question. "How do you explain a grade of *C* in your math class?" She peers down at what must be a copy of my report card in her file.

Will that one blemish on my record keep coming back to scar me? I don't want to tell her I didn't understand because they might think I'm too stupid for McAllen. I wish I could blame Mrs. Vecchionne, but I can't. "Algebra is hard," I say simply, trying not to sound as defensive as I feel, "but I'm working hard to understand it."

Mrs. Biery waits for me to say more, but I don't. She frowns, makes some abrupt marks, and we move on.

It wasn't a total disaster despite Mrs. Biery's question, I think later, as I leave McAllen to catch the bus to my own school. It went fairly well. Anyway, I'm relieved that it's over. I did it! and I feel as great as I felt when I stepped off the train in New York.

I did it. All by myself.

Two weeks later another letter arrives from McAllen.

Dear Mr. and Mrs. Armstrong:

Thank you for your daughter's application to enter the Math and Science Magnet Program at McAllen High School. I regret to inform you, however, that we cannot offer Anne a spot in our 1972 entering class.

We hear from dozens of bright and talented young people like your daughter, and our decisions are very tough ones to make. Please know that it was a pleasure meeting Anne at her interview, and we wish her the best as she pursues her goals.

Sincerely,

George E. Stokes, Principal

16

I'm still curled into a ball on the living room sofa, my eyes red and swollen hard, when Mama gets home. I point to the hateful letter banished to the floor. Mama reads it, almost chokes asking me what it means. "When did they meet you? What interview?" Through sobs, I confess that I went on my own and why.

"You're always saying you have to be the one to take off from work. So I was gonna ask Daddy, but he—"

"Oh, Annie!" she wails. "How could you think—?"

"—would've said no anyway."

Mama reads the letter again. "Annie, we'd have done anything—*anything*."

I collapse into tears on the sofa, the disappointment in her voice wrenching my heart. Mama stands over me with her arms limp, like she can't think what to say or do. Finally, she sits down, hugs me, and lets me cry for as long as I want. "It's okay, Annie. It's all right."

It's not all right. I didn't make it. They don't want me. Just like I thought from the very beginning: I'm not smart enough. Why did Mr. Appleberry ever think they would want me? How will I face him? Everybody in the class? How have I fooled everybody for so long? Grandmother and Clarice think I'm chosen. Ha ha, what a joke. My parents, all my teachers, Sue—they all think I'm so smart. It's all been a great big joke on them.

Pale Hecate's words haunt me. Annie Armstrong is a failure. An egghead who can't even get into Egghead High.

There is no painless way to face the truth in Enriched Science the next day, so I just tell them straight out, "I didn't get in." It sounds even worse coming after the news that Michael, Isa, and Ralph got their McAllen acceptance letters on the same day my rejection came. Shane and Shawn hadn't even applied because they know they want to play basketball at Walker. So that means the only one they rejected was me.

"I'm really sorry for you," Michael says, not even sounding sincere. I sit rigidly, trying to hold back tears. I'm angry at Michael, but more at myself for being so crushed. So I didn't get in. It's Egghead High, after all. Who wants to go there!

I do.

Mr. Appleberry gives my shoulder a reassuring squeeze and goes on teaching the class.

———

I have to go to school, of course, but nothing anybody can do or say will get me out of my room otherwise.

One weekend Mama offers, "I'll drive you to the library. Or, I know, a movie. Come on, we'll all go together."

"No thank you," I tell her politely.

"Annie, you can't just mope around here all the time."

"But my ears still hurt." They don't, but it's a convenient excuse. I've got a whole litany of excuses for moping around, but Mama doesn't want to hear them.

One weekend Clarice calls. "Guess what, Annie. The baby's due soon."

"That's great, Clarice," I reply, unable to muster enthusiasm, even for her.

"You don't sound impressed."

"I know. I guess I haven't thought about it."

Mama put Clarice up to calling me, I figure, because she eventually gets around to telling me, "Annie, don't let this one thing get you down. Remember what we talked about when you were here. I have faith in you, Annie girl."

I catch the tail ends of conversations, my parents whispering in other rooms, no doubt sharing their disappointment in me. I've depressed all of us with my failure. Daddy doesn't know whether to be angry at me or sympathetic. One evening when he gets home from work, he says, "You're worrying your mama to death."

"I do all my chores and my studying," I tell him, keeping *what more do you want?* to myself.

"Still, she's worried." He stops then and looks at me for a while. Suddenly, his expression shifts from scolding to sympathy. "I'm sorry, baby girl," Daddy says, his voice breaking. He looks for a moment like he's going to cry, and that shocks me.

His head hangs, and he looks tired and old, and, I don't know—empty. Deflated. I want to reach out and hug him because he looks so sad it almost makes me forget my own pain. He tells me, "I'm doing my best, Annie. I'm working hard."

"I know you are, Daddy," I say. I'm not sure I do know what he's talking about. Why must he work two jobs? Where do we spend so much money?

He goes to his own room and falls into an exhausted sleep.

I speak nicely to everybody, and I do what I am told, but mostly I keep to myself. If my room before was like a cocoon, now it is more like a coffin.

Then, one afternoon in February, a phone call brings me back to the land of the living.

A deep, preacher-sounding voice asks to speak to Mr. or Mrs. Armstrong. "They're unavailable," I reply, what I've been trained to say when my parents are not home. "May I take a message?"

"Is this Annie?" the voice asks. Taken off guard, I reply yes before I remember that this is a stranger and I'm not to give out information over the telephone.

"Well, you're just the person I'm trying to reach."
Immediately, I get chills, thrilled by what he's saying
and the way he sounds, like I'd won a contest or something. "My name is Lorenzo Woolfolk. I'm an attorney.
I'm also executor for the estate of Otis Blackstone." I
almost drop the telephone at the mention of Mr. Blackstone's name. My heart thuds heavily against my chest,
so loudly that I miss a few of his next words. ". . . to
my office next week for the reading of his will."

"Excuse me?" I interrupt.

He says, "Have your parents call me, please, Annie.
It's very important." He tells me his number and I write
it down. Before he hangs up, he asks, "Do you know
the telephone number of a Lila Tippet? Amanda Blackstone didn't have that one."

I recite the number automatically. I know it better
than I know my own. The lawyer thanks me and hangs
up, leaving me wondering what there could be in Mr.
Blackstone's will that concerns the Tippets and me.

Money? A fortune? Did Mr. Blackstone leave us an
inheritance just like the long-lost uncles do in movies?
Excited, I dial their number. It's busy, so I call my
mother at work.

"Hold onto your horses," Mama warns. "It's probably
just some little token of his appreciation. Mr. Blackstone
wasn't a millionaire, you know."

"But his family owned their own business. And all
that land around his house."

"Still," Mama interrupts, "it's probably some item
from the home. Maybe the piano," she adds wistfully.

I stop to consider that. Mama is probably right. Mr. Blackstone knew how much we admired his wife's concert grand piano. Maybe I could even take lessons again, like I used to do. Sometimes I miss them, even though I hated to practice on the church piano. But as I hang up, I still think that there is something more to it. Maybe it's not a fortune. Maybe it's no money at all. Just the idea that someone has included my name in his last will and testament is enough to make me forget for the moment about being depressed. I call the Tippets again.

"Did he call you?" I ask Sue.

"Sure did," Sue replies. "Doesn't he sound like a serious Fudgsicle?"

"Did he tell you?"

"But he's maybe more of a Supreme, like his son."

"Like what son?"

"Isa. Isa Woolfolk."

"That's Isa's father? Oh, of course—the lawyer!"

The whole event is becoming even more mysterious and fun. "Gee, Sue. Wonder what it's all about?"

"You think he left us something, Annie?" Sue asks.

I take in and let out a deep breath. "Maybe."

She hangs up to call Claude at work. A few minutes later, my telephone rings again.

"Annie?"

My breath catches. "Claude."

Just the sound of his voice, cracking a little when he asks, "Is it true?" is enough to make me smile. After all the months of missing him, the pain melts at the end of a telephone line. But I keep my cool.

"We won't know that until we get there, will we?"

He says, "Aren't you excited?"

"Ye-es," I say, drawing out the word. "I am. 'Bye, Claude," I say and hang up.

For the first time in a long time, I feel a Cheshire cat grin spreading across my face.

The elevator to the fifth floor of Mr. Woolfolk's downtown office building rides so smoothly you feel nothing after the initial jolt, even when it stops. In the narrow hallway we pass office doors with opaque glass windows. On one, the stenciled letters read, "Dr. Beauregard, Optometrist." Another, "Pax Employment Agency." The third door down, number 505, says, "Lorenzo Woolfolk, Esq." Daddy stops before it, unsure whether to knock or just go in. Mama and I look at each other and back at him with no answer. He tries the knob and it opens easily into a small reception room.

A woman's voice says good morning. A lady wearing a two-piece suit, a white blouse, and an Afro gets up from behind a desk, extending her hand with a smile. "I'm Jacqueline Ross, Mr. Woolfolk's secretary."

Daddy introduces us. Miss Ross says, "You're the first to arrive. We're waiting for—" she checks a steno pad on her desk. "Mrs. Lila Tippet, Claude Tippet, Mrs. Evangeline Jones—"

"Miss Eva—" I blurt out. Miss Ross looks up. I smile

weakly and retreat behind a magazine from the side table.

Miss Ross goes on. "—and, of course, Amanda Blackstone."

As soon as my parents sit next to me, and Miss Ross goes back to her desk, I whisper, "Why is Miss Evangeline gonna be here?"

"We don't know." Mama tells me to be quiet about it. But I notice she and Daddy exchange worried looks.

"It must mean she won. She gets Mr. B.'s house. It's not—" I start to say "fair," but realize how silly that sounds. "—any of my business."

Miss Evangeline bustles in. "Sara! Slim!" she says, as if she's surprised to see *them* here. As usual, she ignores me. "Oh, dear, am I late?"

Miss Ross steps in and assures Miss Evangeline that she's early and asks her to take a seat. Miss Evangeline doesn't seem too pleased to be given directions from the younger woman. She huffs a little but sits down.

Warily, Miss Ross says, "Would anyone like coffee?"

"Oh, yes," Mama and Daddy say.

Miss Evangeline turns her face up and orders, "Sanka, please." Miss Ross nods politely, but I see her roll her eyes as she turns away. I grin again. It feels good to grin.

Soon, Claude and Mrs. Tippett arrive and then Amanda. Miss Ross picks up her telephone, talks into it. Seconds later a tall man opens the inner office door. He is the most gorgeous man you could ever imagine.

He looks like Isa, only better. He looks like an *Ebony* model. He looks like a movie actor. He smiles at me, and I think I will be unable to walk, but my legs get me to a seat in his office where I hold on like I'm on a roller-coaster ride.

Mr. Woolfolk takes his seat. "Thank you all for coming today," he begins, opening a leather-bound folder.

"As you know, this will has been contested by Miss Evangeline Jones, based upon a verbal agreement she claims Mr. Blackstone made before his death." Surreptitiously, we all look at her, all but Amanda, who seems remarkably poised for someone who just might lose her home. Then Mr. Woolfolk says, "Yesterday, a judge ruled against her motion. Therefore, the balance of Mr. Blackstone's estate, after all settlements of taxes, expenses, and the provisions of this will, will be the life estate of Miss Amanda Blackstone."

It takes a few moments for all of us to understand what this means, but when we look at the smile on Amanda's face, we know she has won. Claude cheers and I slap five with him, but everyone else just tries to hide their jubilation with sympathy for Miss Evangeline. For her part, she keeps her eyes on Mr. Woolfolk. He reads on: "Miss Blackstone has entered into an agreement with the Oakwood Restoration Project, under the direction of Miss Evangeline Jones, that since One Oakwood Place is being recognized as a historic monument by the local historical society, she will gladly cooperate with their efforts for the proper restoration of said residence. And when the Blackstone Museum is established, she will serve as chief hostess and continue to live in the residence until such time of her death, when the deed will revert to the Oakwood Restoration Project."

Miss Evangeline looks around at us triumphantly, but we all know Amanda's good will is responsible for things working out this way. If Miss Evangeline had had her way, Amanda's title would be "Last Known Resident."

Amanda will make a great hostess. Nobody will get away with anything in that house while she's there.

"Now," Mr. Woolfolk interjects into our gaiety, settling us down. "There is one other provision in this will. I'd like to continue."

We sit back in our chairs like we're watching a play, yet somehow, even though we're in the audience, we're a part of the drama. Mr. Woolfolk clears his throat, but I can see a smile playing around under his mustache.

"Article Two: To Mr. and Mrs. Armstrong, parents of Matthew and Annie, and to Mrs. Lila Tippet, widow and mother of Heath, Claude, Gretchen Susanne, Dorothy, and Cheron, I leave these words:

"You have given the world jewels—your children— and you have been entrusted with their care and nurturing. It is an awesome responsibility, which the three of you have handled well, through struggle together, Slim and Sara, and on your own, Lila.

"You are the people my grandparents and parents envisioned would build and own this community. You are constructing a future for your children, not with bricks and mortar, but with encouragement, education, love, and support. I leave you a scholarship trust fund to send through college those of your children who desire and work hard to attain a university education at the school of their choice."

We nearly hop out of our seats. "What? For college? For us?"

"To Annie and Claude—" Mr. Woolfolk continues, "you brought an old man into the new world. Your vigor and enthusiasm for life and all it has to offer made my last years some of the most pleasant in my life. You will understand why I will call this endowment the Lizette Blackstone Scholarship Fund, and why I designate that your expenses be paid through graduate and/or professional study so that there is no financial limit ever to what you can achieve.

"Claude, Annie, understand this: To those to whom much is given, much is expected.

"Finally, to all my newfound friends, neighbors, and especially to my dear niece Amanda, daughter of my brother and daughter to me: Do not mourn me, but be happy, for I have joined my dear Lizette and we are young again."

We sniff back tears, some of us, and some of us, like my mother, just go ahead and cry.

Mr. Woolfolk refolds the papers and looks happy and relieved. The more I look at him, the more I think about Isa. I can't wait to get back to school.

Mama and Daddy are in a celebratory mood. Daddy says, "Let's take the whole day off, Sara, and take our daughter to lunch." Mama doesn't even hesitate, so we go to Rilke's Department Store's restaurant on the top floor. I order French onion soup. Mama goes, "Mmmm mmm," with what she considers a French accent.

"I had some in New York," I say casually.

We talk about Mr. Blackstone's will like it's a Christmas gift. "I can't believe it, Annie. Your college paid for—" Daddy says. "I may never have to drive a cab again!"

"Such lovely words of encouragement," Mama puts in, threatening to cry again.

Wait a minute, I think, ignoring Mama's gushing for what Daddy just said. "Drive a cab? You mean you've been driving a cab at night to pay for my college?"

"Why sure," Daddy says proudly. "Saved up a little bit. Not much. But now—no worries! You got it made, Annie! You can go wherever you want!"

He sounds like he's accepting that idea for the first time. Mama sits there nodding. My mind races ahead to the time when I can maybe go live in New York and attend NYU. Or maybe I'll apply to Harvard. Why not! Why—?

A dreadful realization cracks through my euphoria. "What college will want me? I'm too dumb even to get into McAllen High School!"

They look at me, perplexed and silent in the face of

my sudden tears. How can I keep being such a disappointment when everybody's trying so hard to help me?

Daddy sputters, "Don't cry, Annie." I keep bawling, not caring that other diners are staring at us. "Don't cry, baby girl. We'll take care of it."

Then he hits the table and says to Mama, "Sara, we got to do something about this."

He stands up. Mama says, "Slim?"

He fishes around in his pocket, pulling out a dime. "I'm gonna get some answers from those McAllen people before this day is out. Here they got our daughter thinking she ain't good enough. We know that ain't true. I want to know why they turned my baby down."

"Slim, what's gotten into you?"

"Mr. Blackstone is right, Sara. Annie's our responsibility. Here these people have turned her down and got her doubting herself, and we don't even know why. We've never even met them. Never talked to them. Well, I'ma talk to somebody and somebody's gonna tell me why. And they better have a good reason, or I'm gonna raise all kind of trouble!"

"You can't just go charging down there," Mama frets.

I'm alert again, no tears. "Please go, Daddy," I urge, squeezing into their argument.

"See there!" he exclaims.

Mama makes some more noises, but Daddy goes to find the telephone.

I do want to know why they rejected me, but mostly I want to see my father go down there and kick butt.

17

Daddy must've sounded pretty convincing, or pretty angry, on the telephone because Mr. Stokes told him we could come to McAllen right away.

In Mr. Stokes's office, Daddy sits on the edge of his seat, his voice level, but his emotions clear. "If she was one of your top candidates, sir, then tell me why she won't be coming here next year."

Mr. Stokes looks uncomfortable. "Mr. and Mrs. Armstrong," he begins, lacing his fingers together atop his desk. "It has to do with certain intangible factors that are often hard to explain." He clears his throat. I watch my parents. Daddy keeps his eyes on Mr. Stokes's.

"It seemed that your daughter was lacking the . . . supportive environment our students need to be successful here at McAllen. Our program is a tough one, Mr. and Mrs. Armstrong, and our students need all the help they can get. Your daughter showed up for her interview all alone. In addition, her math grade had fallen last term. We felt, well, we wondered whether there was, er, there was enough support in her home, whether she could handle the pressures of going here."

I hold my breath, finally realizing how colossal my mistake—coming here alone—actually was. These people thought my parents didn't care about me. Maybe I thought that too.

Daddy blinks his eyes several times, looks at Mama (whose face is set like stone). He turns back to Mr. Stokes. "Let me tell you about a supportive environment, sir. This child—our daughter—made all the arrangements for her interview, found her way here all by herself, and completed an interview before three strangers on her own. You can't produce such an independent, confident child unless she has a supportive environment."

Mama nods.

"We're working people, Mr. Stokes, both of us. We have to be. Annie was only three or four when her mother had to return to work. I was on the night shift at that time. Her mother would be fixing Annie's breakfast when I got home in the morning. Off Sara would go, and I'd take over, but by afternoon, you can understand, I needed to sleep.

"I could sit Annie up on the bed with Mr. Webster's dictionary and nod off as she sat there. She'd turn to the page for cat and say, "c-a-t, cat, *meow*," then she'd turn to dog, spell it, and say, "*ruff, ruff.*" She wouldn't stop there. She'd turn to tiger and lion and monkey and even elephant. I could hear her in my sleep.

"Her mother taught her to read before she started kindergarten. Taught her how to multiply her numbers up to the ten times table. Taught her to dress and feed herself, how to talk to people nicely and do as she was told. Even now, even though she's working, she's calling, giving Annie instructions. On any day in our neighborhood, Annie can play outside and every adult around will know what she's up to. Do you understand what I mean, sir? We're very much a part of Annie's life. Our daughter has all the support she needs. She's got support you can't even imagine. Why, one of our leading citizens just left her a scholarship in his will. You hear that, Mr. Stokes? She's got *money*."

Daddy sits back in his chair. "Don't you worry about my daughter being out here adrift. She ain't, and she won't ever be."

I don't remember reading the dictionary and barking like a dog. But it must have happened. A lot of things go on that I don't know about, like Mama and Daddy sending that extra money to New York, like Mr. Blackstone rewriting his will, so he could keep on helping us after he was gone. All this time I've been thinking that I'm walking alone across a tightrope, when really, there's this invisible net spread out underneath me.

Mr. Stokes looks impressed with Daddy's speech and even with my explanation about my math grade and the fact that I work after school with Mrs. Vecchionne two days a week. But we leave McAllen with no promises.

They've made their decisions, so as far as that's concerned, nothing's changed. But then again, I've discovered that even when it seems like nothing's changed, something's *always* changing.

I learn in Enriched Science the next day that only Michael and Isa will be attending McAllen. Ralph Singleton's parents have decided to send him to a private school. No public school, not even McAllen, is good enough for old Ralphy.

I tell the class about my "second interview" and try not to feel sorry for myself.

Mr. Appleberry says I should apply again next year. "You will show them that you are determined, that you don't give up easily. You will show how much you value their program and your future. Once you're accepted, you may have to catch up, Miss Armstrong. But I'll be here with any help you need."

So that's what I'm going to do.

Mr. Appleberry announces that he wants us to work in pairs on our second science project. He says a lot of the world's great scientists worked in teams. I act casual when Isa asks me if I will work with him, but if he could X-ray my insides, he'd see all my organs jumping for joy.

We meet after school to discuss our project.

"What do you want to do?" Isa asks as we sit together at a cafeteria table. I try not to stare into his eyes, so dark and steady.

I consider trying some of Sue's flirting techniques,

but I'm afraid he'll just look at me like I'm crazy. We've been together in class almost every day since school started, but we've never talked about anything except science and math.

I decide to keep my interest to myself and my mind on the subject at hand, our project. "Well, what are you interested in?" I inquire, pen in hand to take notes.

To my surprise, he pulls the pen right out of my hand and writes across the lines of my open notebook, "You."

If Isa had written an entire novel in French right before my eyes he couldn't have astonished me more than he did with that one word.

Since then, we've been talking every day, mostly about how sad it is that we'll be at different schools next year.

Claude calls me one Sunday. "Come run with me today, Annie."

"I don't like running, Claude."

He is quiet for a long moment. Then he says, "Well, just come out and talk?"

For months I have wanted to hear him say that, wanted to talk to Claude about everything that has gone on since we argued last fall. I agree to meet and walk to the park.

Winter's holding on tightly. The temperature's around thirty-eight degrees, and the sky's still cloudy. But birds dot the ground in Prospect Park, pecking across frozen ground, here and there finding a soft spot.

It's too cold to stand still or sit down, so Claude and I walk easily around the track. "Will you keep working, now that college is paid for?"

He doesn't hesitate a second. "Sure. Mr. Hershey's getting old. He needs me to take over sometimes. I practically run that store."

"Um hm," I say quietly, enjoying a good old Claude boast. I didn't expect he'd stop working. And with track season coming up, he'll be busier than ever. I keep asking questions, bracing myself for each expected answer.

"Do you have a girlfriend, Claude?"

"Yeah," he says after a while.

It doesn't kill me. I think about Isa.

Claude stops walking. "Can we still be friends, you know, like we used to be?"

I've thought about this since seeing Claude in the lawyer's office. When we slapped hands together over Amanda's victory, it felt good, like we were already friends again, without having to say it. It was like we'd picked up a game we used to play and continued it as if nothing had happened in between. But a lot has happened—has changed.

I look Claude straight in the eye. Some things have to be said. "I'm sorry—I mean it—for what I said that time."

"Forget it, Annie," Claude graciously tells me. "I was mad because it was true. No way could I pay for college on forty dollars a week." He laughs. "And now—"

"And now—" I repeat. We slap five for Mr. Blackstone and his scholarship.

"Still, I shouldn't have said it. It's just—" I've decided to come clean with him. "I was—just—"

"What, what?" he urges.

"Fine!" I exclaim. "I was so in love with you that all I could think about was that your going to college meant leaving me."

"What do you mean *was*? Aren't you still in love with me, Annie?" Claude asks, grinning.

"Yes," I say, then follow after a pause with, "and *no*."

He looks at me. He understands. "Friends?" He's still smiling, that Claude look, which used to make me dizzy.

Used to.

"You know it."

We hug each other and finish our walk.

Hey, Annie." This is my brother's voice on the telephone, but he sounds so different at first I almost don't recognize him. "You there by yourself?"

"You know they're sitting on that sofa, watching television. It's eight-thirty on a Sunday night. Where else would they be?"

Mama and Daddy are in the living room, but I had been in the kitchen, gazing with pride at the science project Isa and I completed. Isa likes to design and make things (he wants to be an architect), so we decided on a project that required us to build something. He sketched it, and together one day after school we went to his garage and put together a ramp and a runway out of pieces of wood and some smooth rubber track from an old raceway toy he had. Isa made the angle of the ramp adjustable, and we sent toy cars, rubber balls, empty cans, full cans—objects of different mass, anything we could find that would roll—along its path.

We calculated ramp speed and runway speed, acceleration, momentum, and force. We recorded our results and made several charts; from there, I went on to use those same calculations to figure the escape velocity from earth and the speed necessary to carry a fifty-ton rocket from one planet to another in a given amount of time. We got an *A* from Mr. Appleberry for successfully "integrating our interests." Isa got to build; I got to explore space travel. Even Mrs. Vecchionne loved it because our math was correct. Other students liked our project because they could play with it; they could roll and time objects at our display. Best of all, Isa and I had fun working together.

But Matty's calling with his own project to report. "Clarice had the baby, Annie. It's a girl."

"Oh, wow!" I scream, nearly dropping the phone. "A girl!" Superpower Mama is at my side in a second, excitedly yanking the phone away.

"Matty, is it true?" she asks, then breaks into a grin. "How is she? How is Clarice?"

Daddy and I hover close as Mama reports Matty's words. "Born twenty minutes ago. Baby is fine. Ten fingers, ten toes. Clarice is fine. Can't decide on a name. *Don't you dare name her Jazzy!*"

I'm finally given a chance to talk again. "I wish I could be there."

"Me too, sis. But I've taken twenty pictures of her already. I'll send you one in the mail. That'll have to do till we see you again. Maybe this summer."

We agree to arrange it and hang up. The television goes off. Daddy and I talk about the baby while Mama calls everybody she can think of to give them the news.

During the week Matty's picture arrives. When I pull his letter out of the mailbox, another one comes with it. My heart skips and races when I read the return address: McAllen High School.

My hands shake as I open it, standing right there on the porch in my bare feet. I pull it out and read it, fold my hands to my heart, and read it again. *"We have an unexpected opening in our freshman class and after consideration have decided to offer it to Anne. We hope you have not made other arrangements for Anne's high school education, for we think having her here will be mutually beneficial."*

I'm in? I read the letter a third time. *"An unexpected opening?"* Maybe Ralph Singleton's spot. I fall to my knees with gratitude. "Thank you, Ralph," I chant. "Thank your parents for being such snobs. Thank you, God! Thanks, everybody!" I repeat. I feel like I've just won an Oscar. I scream, "Yes! Yes! Yes!" all through the house and into the telephone receiver when I get Mama on the phone. *"I'm going to McAllen!"*

"This is too good to be true," Mama breathes, but I read her the letter and she has to believe it. "We'll have a five-star dinner. A celebration, Annie girl. We have so much to be grateful for." She sniffs back tears.

"Don't cry. Be happy. I'm happy, happy, happy." We finally hang up, but not before I persuade Mama to let me tell Daddy in my own way. She wants to be with me when I tell him, but we both know she'll blurt it out the minute he walks in, and I want to take my time. I've got some other things I want to say to him first. So, later that afternoon when we hear Daddy's key in the lock, she agrees to go upstairs until I break the news.

I wait for him in the kitchen with a glass of crumb-laden milk and a box of graham crackers.

"You want some crackers?" I ask.

Daddy falls into a chair. "You know what, Annie, I think I do. Your mama upstairs?"

I murmur, "Um hm," as I pour him a glass of milk and set some crackers on a napkin in front of him. We dunk the crackers and nibble in silence for a while.

I don't want to tell him just yet. I want to sit here and look at my daddy and watch him eat graham crackers. I want to tell him a whole lot of other things first but don't know where to start. I want to apologize for being such a brat before. I want to thank him for working so hard just for me, just so that I can go to college. I want to thank him for being my daddy.

Oh, what the heck, I'll just tell him.

"Got something to show you." I pause for drama, then pull one letter from under the tablecloth.

"Dear Mr. and Mrs. Armstrong," I begin.

"You got in!"

"Yes!" I scream, throwing my arms around him. We do our little Jackie Gleason dance. "It's because you went down there and told them all off—"

Daddy stops me. "Nah, nah. Whatever I said to that

man wouldn't have made a bit of difference if you hadn't done the work to get there in the first place. I'm so proud of you, Shoopaloop, even though—" He chokes off the rest of his sentence, lets out a big sigh. "—even though I haven't been around much to tell you."

To think, all this time I thought I was the Bizarro one, and here's Daddy apologizing to me.

We settle down, and I show him the second envelope. Inside is a photograph of his first grandchild, my very own niece, a peachy-faced, wide-eyed, curly-haired baby girl. His whole body relaxes into a proud grin and he just stares at the photo for a long time, tears spilling from his eyes. Probably now he'll start working like crazy again to pay for *her* college education. Dads are like that—even though so much is given to us, they'll want to give more.

Underneath the picture, Clarice has written the name she and Matty have finally chosen for this small new addition to our family:

Her name is *Imani Anne*.